UNITY OF CONSCIOUSNESS

Divine Wisdom Manifest Through Physical Form

Through the Mediumship of

Carol Crawford

Note for Librarians: A cataloguing record for this book is available from Library and Archives Canada at www.collectionscanada.ca/amicus/index-e.html

Printed in Victoria, BC, Canada.

ISBN: 978-1-4269-1410-2 (sc)

Our mission is to efficiently provide the world's finest, most comprehensive book publishing service, enabling every author to experience success. To find out how to publish your book, your way, and have it available worldwide, visit us online at www.trafford.com

Trafford rev. 8/5/2009

 www.trafford.com

North America & international
toll-free: 1 888 232 4444 (USA & Canada)
phone: 250 383 6864 ♦ fax: 812 355 0484

...The winds of time has been spoken of much tonight, time is of no consequence to those in the spirit realm, time shifts, time stands still – I started thinking about the physical and that has brought me back, I could feel a tugging, I felt that I had so much to say.

Baal Shem Tov – October 23, 2008

Contents

DEDICATION

PAUL *Artwork by Laura Floyd*

The day that I met Paul was when I was invited to do a clairvoyant reading evening at a beautiful chapel in Geelong, Victoria, Australia. This was a very special building as it had only ever been used as a meeting place for Masons and for spiritual endeavours. As I went to work that night, I was asked if I would give a reading to the occupants who owned the premises, they took me into the baptism room, now this room was like a medieval chapel and in the centre was this pit, this bath-type structure and in the centre of that was this big pillar with a ball on the top like an orb and the water would fill it and all of the lights would go on and the person would stand in there on the steps descending in and they would be baptised.

Now as I was doing the reading, I became aware of a presence walking up and down, up and down and finally when the reading was over and the couple left, I sat down and I said "who are you" and he said "I am Paul and I am here to work with you from now on" From that night on I always got the sense of this person, Paul has a hood and I have come to know him as an ancient Essene High Priest or Noah in that time which was before Christ. He has worked with me on many, many occasions and I see Paul as the lynch pin, the living bridge, that connector piece between all of the other energies, without Paul making that connection and giving that fluid flow of energy and stability to that flow of information, I just don't feel that the information and the energies that are coming through would actually be able to achieve this and that is Paul. He is centrepiece and paramount in the whole process and when I sit for trance it is Paul who I feel wash through me, the face changes and it mimics the expression in the picture above.

From that point it is like he may step back and he allows and works with and brings in all of the other energies, I think the spiritual philosophy has called it the doorkeeper, the keeper of the door between the worlds.

I dedicate this book to PAUL – as Paul said "this book is me, this is my book".

Carol Crawford

FOREWORD

Over the last fifteen years I have been on a journey through the illusions of the physical world, to try to make sense of the world I have always had a window seat into. As far back as I can remember I have lived in "The world of the Spirit" where the unseen world was more real to me than the world in front of my eyes.

As a child I would regularly have visitors that would appear in the darkness. They took two forms either full colour manifestations, where they would sit next to me on my bed and I would feel the bed move under their weight, or a more misty appearance whom I called the misty people, I don't know which ones scared me more.

The more physical ones I thought were real people breaking into our house, of course when I told my parents they would tell me it was just a dream and not to worry, this just confused me more as they were so real I was terrified of them. I needed someone to help me to make some sense of this but I couldn't make anyone around me understand just how real these night visitors were. But the misty ones were even more scary because that was what I had seen on TV Ghosts, and that was a really bad thing, what did they want? Did they want to hurt me? I didn't know, and if you think my more physical visitors were hard to explain, boy these ghosts were even harder to explain. Of course my parents just thought this kid has a wild imagination.

To begin with I told everyone who would listen, my parents, our neighbours even my teachers. I soon learned to keep quiet as people just didn't believe. Eventually my Grandma came up to baby sit for the night, I plucked up the courage to tell her what was happening and she believed me she told me that the same things happened to her but from now on I wasn't to speak of it because people couldn't accept it. Then she told me how to quiet it down and block it out because I had to live in the world and as I grew up I could learn more about it but for now she put it to sleep.

Of course I didn't understand what she was doing at the time, but years later I found myself the grown up and my baby boys in the same situation and yes that's right I used my grandmas wisdom to help my kids. It's funny you know this really does run in families.

As I said thing quieted down until I was about fourteen, I was sitting on a bench at school I was always known to my family as the daydreamer and the overly relaxed one of the kids. I could lie down and space out from the world as easily as speaking, I would go the most amazing journeys into my mind and meet and speak to these light beings, they were my friends and would share things with me, I now know I was meditating, but I never told anyone because of my earlier experience.

Anyway around fourteen years old, I was sitting on the bench just dreaming away when I became aware of the most amazing bright light and colour around all the other kids in the yard. Even the trees were shimmering in this sea of light and colour, I was entranced by the beauty, there was no fear I just felt safe. In that instant the way I saw the world changed whenever and wherever I looked I could see this light it was around people, animals, trees, even objects like seats, tables everything was light filled. This went on over the next few years, I just assumed everyone was seeing what I was so it never occurred to tell anyone until one day I was sitting with my twin sister, Joy, in front of a mirror and as usual there was that light around her head, only this time I told her what I was seeing and yes she was seeing the same things it's funny neither one had thought to tell the other because we had just assumed everyone saw this.

As we sat looking at each others reflection in the mirror we decided to play a game with it. So we sat and concentrated very hard and began to tell each other exactly what it was we could see around each other. All of a sudden I became aware of a human shape building up to the side of her head I could see the hair, face and shoulders it was so real, as I began to describe this to her she said the same was around me and it was getting clearer and clearer for both of us.

I had to know what I was seeing it seemed so familiar to me a bit like you know that you have seen it before but cant quite recall where, my sister had the same experience.

I had to find out what was happening to us, I thought the best place to start was the bible. Now as I had never had any religious practice I had no idea what I was reading about I couldn't make any sense of this book. I tried and tried to understand what I was reading but it just didn't make any sense to me. Over the following years on and off I would read things in magazines but felt very perplexed and frustrated at the lack of information available to me, it was about this time that my mother became very sick, we had just come home from a holiday when she was diagnosed with bowel cancer. At fifteen I was devastated and so frightened I was going to lose my mum. We didn't lose mum as she made a full recovery and has never looked back but that kick started her on a bit of an investigation into what happens to us when we die. Mum started to go to clairvoyant readings, and was given information on a tape that actually happened within six months.

Mum decided that we girls should go too so off we went, this opened up a door into understanding myself like I had never felt before. There were people who were explaining what I had been experiencing all of my life **(I Wasn't Mad)** this was real. I wasn't imagining it. We continued to go and learn for a few more years until the group stopped, but at least I knew what I could see was real that allowed me to relax and with that I continued to carve out my life in this world doing all the things teenagers do. My sister and I would go out to nightclubs and party, when she met this man named Peter.

He was a medium and dabbled on the Ouija board. He told her about Guardian spirits and trance mediumship, he told her that she could be a trance medium, but there was something just not right with him my sister was very frightened by him and what he was doing.

It wasn't long before she moved away from him, but he had given her a book written by Dawn Hill. She gave me the book to read and all I can say that is when for the first time I could finally understand who I was. I was a medium so I did what I was reading and started to meditate everyday at the same time to make that connection stronger and by doing that spirit would know where I would be at that time so they could make their presence felt and I could feel and hear them.

This went on for a few months with nothing earth shattering happening, then one day I was lying there and I hear this voice shout in my ear. It was a Scottish accent. Which wasn't so surprising as I am Scottish after all. With this I became aware of this presence when I was in that relaxed state. I began to recognise the features and how this presence felt, only now when I meditated my body seemed to become lighter and more sensitive to its surroundings. I continued to read everything I could lay my hands on and the flow of information I was receiving became stronger, I was seeing pictures and hearing voices and getting information before it happened.

A few more years passed and I got married and had my first son I was now 24 years old and had been busy with life, my sister was also married, Joy and her husband joined a development group. I was asked to go for an interview to see if I wanted to join this group. I call this my apprenticeship. I was taught how to receive messages and more importantly how to present this information to the public. I practiced and went on public platform through the Spiritualist churches. I had two boys by then and my marriage was falling apart. I fell into a depression and went through some of the hardest times of my life. Again like the guardian angel that she is my sister came to the rescue and gave me a tape by the author Caroline Myss, called "The Creation of Health".

I sat down in my darkest despair and was moved to my very foundations. At the end of that tape I said a prayer God help me if I am not meant to be in this marriage then set me free. That was in December 1998 and by January my marriage was over. It was a terrible divorce and took years to move through the courts and anger between my ex and myself. All the time I was reading Caroline Myss and listening to her tapes.

The dark night of the soul was one that helped me to understand where I was and gave me some direction on how to change and empower myself to let go of the past and move into my future. It is now 2007.

Two years ago I was sitting in front of my computer and for quite a while the thought that one day I might write a book to do with spirit and working with spirit and helping to teach people about what I had been working with and learning as a medium in that field. I was writing and I always believed that when I wrote that I was trancing, I was bringing through spirit and they were putting the words in my mind and I was just copying them on the computer and quite often what would come through I would have no preconceived ideas about, however, this day I was impressed by spirit. It said, you will be the teacher of the ninth centre.

Now the ninth centre, I was so excited that literally I couldn't contain myself, I remember jumping up and saying "how fabulous, I will be the teacher of the ninth centre" and like a little kid who wakes up on Christmas morning, you know the excitement, all of a sudden it occurred to me – what is the ninth centre, I have no idea. I then realised that it would take a couple of years or more for me to actually catch up with that little bit of inspiration that spirit shared with me and truly, this book is those two years in the making. From that moment as I worked doors just opened up.

I had always had an issue doing trance work but all of a sudden it became very clear that this was exactly how I was meant to be working and for the first time in the whole of my life I recognised myself as a trance medium. As those two years went by I began to work more and more in the field and as I worked people would be sent and this whole new reality began to open and I began to see the world in a very different order and all through those years it never occurred to me that this was the book in the making. It wasn't until Alex and Mary Moon approached me and said would you like to do some trance sessions? Mary was happy to transcribe out what is brought through from spirit. It is almost like the moment that I said yes I truly met all of the different aspects of myself who I had known were probably there but could never have said it, recognised it or spoke it, a door opened and all of the preceding years of work fell and fitted into the trance sessions that we were now sharing, it is a sacred time.

I believe as do Alex and Mary and my partner Kevin that what is coming through and what we are sharing with you today is a truth so profound that it will take you in to a totally different reality from the world that you have been experiencing today. There is knowledge that is so vast, I believe that you don't even have to open this book at the beginning and read through it, I believe that at any time anybody could pick up this book, open it up and be able to understand that day's trance session and it would bring some kind of knowledge. Maybe it will help us to make sense of a world which we quite often don't fully understand, that we fear and I think that the world of the spiritual realities, the spiritual consciousness that lives within all of us, that voice that we don't listen to, intuition, I think it is trying to reach out and help us to understand a world gone crazy and the information in these pages, understand and know that they are not brought through from a mind of the physical earth, they are shared with a spiritual reality, spiritual beings.

It is truly an honour to receive these beings, so you read the book and you make up your mind as to whether and ordinary human person can know this truth with such clarity and then you make up your mind as to how you feel about it because the most important thing is knowing that this is your journey and the words on the page have been sent to you by an eternal ever loving source.

Carol Crawford

ACKNOWLEDGEMENTS

I have to say that I didn't really believe in my own ability and it was certain people who came into my life, and, I believe had been Heaven sent, who have always stood behind me in my quest to understand spirituality and my own mediumship.

First of all, I would like to say thank you to my partner Kevin for without his loving support and unconditional belief in my abilities and in me I would never have had the courage to pursue this path but more than that he gave me the support financially and physically so that I could devote my time to working with matters of the spirit.

To my twin sister when in the early years I had very little confidence, she was the one behind me giving me a swift kick up the backside every time I said "I can't do it" when she knew that I could but it takes a lot of self and self confidence to actually stand up and work in this field of mediumship. So Joy I would like to thank you especially because throughout my whole life you have been my best friend and confidante, you always believed in me, and have always stood behind me, and been there to guide me and without your belief in me, I would never have managed to achieve what I have achieved in regards to my connection with spirit – so Joy, thank you.

My parents, instead of seeing me as odd, a bit strange perhaps eccentric, even though I unnerved and upset them at times with

the mediumship and the connection to spirit, they always accepte
me and loved me and I will always thank them for that and the
have always supported me.

Now to the two people who made this possible – I woul
like to say thank you to Mary and Alex Moon. Alex has a thirs
for knowledge and a logical brain where he can put all of the
different information into a format and create the book, the
writing, without that I could never have achieved this book.
Mary, of course, she is the typist and has lovingly sat chained to
the computer hour after hour, month after month transcribing
the words that are brought through from spirit.

So you see, this is not my book, this is a book that is written
on the love and belief and the compassion and the spirit and the
hard work of all of us who have been a part of it. I am eternally
grateful to everybody for all of their help and helping me to
achieve my dream of being of service to spirit.

Carol Crawford

INTRODUCTION

Mary and I sat in awe and wonderment as each of the trance sessions was recorded. Carol *"stepped aside"* and allowed each entity to speak through her and the personality and individual characteristics of each became evident as the sessions progressed.

Paul was strong and powerful yet compassionate and loving. Lilong Li was soft and gentle and given to gesticulating with graceful hand movements to emphasise points. There was much love and compassion for each of us as each entity spoke with feeling. On occasions Carol's features took on an Angelic expression as the entity spoke with great love.

In the early sessions Mary and I were a little overwhelmed in the presence of the entities. But as the sessions progressed we became more relaxed in their presence and thus became able to chat with them as if they were old friends. They almost became human or did we become more like spirit.

Very little of the dialogue has been altered or edited except that some personal comments, which were not related to the overall message of "Unity of Consciousness", were deleted. The dialogue has been faithfully transcribed to the written word as it was spoken. I am impressed in that very few corrections to grammar or syntax were needed.

As the names of the entities came to light Mary was impressed to research to discover if indeed these entities actually did have incarnations hence the inclusion of the small historical section. The internet provides extensive information regarding "ancient" times.

Mary and I feel privileged and honoured to have been part of this process over the latter part of 2008 and into early 2009 for we have gained a greater knowledge and understanding of life from every aspect. We also feel blessed that Carol allowed us into her life for it has been an amazing journey in learning more about ourselves as spirit and human.

We hope that you, the reader, gains as much knowledge and understanding about life from reading about this wonderful experience as we gained from putting it together.

Love and light,

Alex Moon.

If I keep thinking what I have always thought,
Then I will keep doing what I have always done.
If I keep doing what I have always done,
Then I will keep getting what I have always got.

Author unknown

THE ENTITIES

CAROL'S IMPRESSIONS

PAUL feels strong and serious, he feels like he will take no nonsense and will get straight to the point. I always have a feeling with him that my energy is moving really fast and he wants to keep it running very quickly and very efficiently, he is efficient, he is organising and he takes charge of the whole situation and he has a depth of wisdom about him. I feel like I am in the bottom of a pool, not of water but of wisdom and it is that depth and intensity of him.

SHISHILA - when Shishila comes in she is radiant, she makes me feel like I could jump up and I could truly create anything that I wanted to. Shishila makes me feel passion and makes me feel inspired - I feel that if someone wanted to have a baby I could go zap, hold their belly and it is done. The energy with her feels like it could move the mountain, she could really create, she feels like the creative being of the river of humanity and there is also the sense that she will guide you through to meet your spirit, to meet the other side of you, it is like she is the door - it is not Paul who is the doorkeeper, it is Shishila. It is like they walk through her radiant light archway to meet Paul who anchors you, there are two steps in that.

The Lady of the Light will guide you and I get the feeling

that with her you also get the energy of Michael, I don't know if they are separate, I don't feel that they are the same but I get the feeling that Michael takes care of lost souls and gets them over into the Light, Michael works to get them into Shishila's light and Michael was given to me years and years ago, whatever Michael is it is does not matter, his name is Michael and that is his job as I work as a medium. I feel that Michael is in the background with this Light and working on that level and I meet him when I am working clearing and cleansing energies.

LILONG LI - when he comes in he tends to be soft, quietly spoken, slow - I want to feel, whereas Paul wants to articulate and makes it feel like it is coming in through the mind and he is very intellectual, Lilong Li wants to feel the energy, he wants you to feel the words that are coming through, very emotional, very warm and very much tapped into feeling the words inside you. Paul doesn't care if you feel the words as long as you get what he is saying, that is all he cares about whereas Lilong Li wants you to take a moment to feel what they are bringing through.

FATHER BARTHOLOMEW is very stoic and is very set in his ways, he would have had a fixed belief on life when he was on the earth, he would take the dictation, he would dot all the i's and cross all of the t's, he was fastidious and he paid attention to detail. He is making sure that all of the information is placed in a way that could be really recognised and understood so he is making sure that all of the components of all of the sessions are put together in the appropriate order but it is more than that, it is like he builds the philosophy, he builds that book, he creates that book, that's the philosophy of it, the foundation of it and that is because he is so fastidious. He was a Father in life as a monk because he liked that discipline, he liked the formation of the religion and the philosophy and the structure, that's what he wanted, that's what he needed when he was on the earth and he would fix his view of that on that philosophy that he was living at that time.

BAAL SHEM TOV is a title and there are a lot of essences that fall under that vibration. Baal Shem Tov feels like he is a leader, he moves people in a direction, he is very inspiring, he is light, he lifts my spirits to the point where he feels like I can actually do it and I can do it because I don't have to believe in the old structure, I can adapt the old structure. He is like a link, like a bridge, he takes all of the wonders of all of the philosophies that have been placed into the earth because when a truth is a truth it is a truth forever and he bridges that into the next incarnation of it on the earth - that is the energy he brings in and that is why he is so integral in these sessions because we are taking a lot of information that has probably been around and said and thrown around but he wants to create that link that brings it into its own essence - that is what Baal Shem Tov worked to create while he was on the earth.

WINSTON WHITEHORSE is very arty in his nature, he wants to thread the words like a poet, he wants to scribe it, tell the story and he wants to pontificate about it, he feels aloof, he feels regal, he always feels like he has a hat on his head and it is a big hat and he has the Shakespearean beard and he would be a deep, deep thinker, he would think about things before he would come through and actually speak about them. He always makes me feel that I would like to rub my chin when he is pondering these deep essence meanings of the Universe; I feel like he is weaving a story, he is telling you the story.

THOTH - I felt this omnipresence, I just felt totally expansive and unlimited, I also felt that I could have broken the law of gravity and limitation, I felt that I could change matter, I just felt that there was no limitation or restriction with this person, just a huge knowing of all knowledge of all traditions. He felt like if he walked into the room you would want to drop to your knees because you could not stand in his presence, he was awe-inspiring and you had such a lot of respect and you just felt like you loved him. He feels like he can stare into your soul and see every part -

you can hide nothing, you are laid open before his feet and I felt that I couldn't breathe in his presence like I was standing before God but it wasn't God, I got a sense of a presence and I don't think God has a presence like the threads of time.

MARY'S IMPRESSIONS

PAUL has a very strong character and He is very wise and knowledgeable. He is forthright (would not put up with any nonsense) and somewhat serious. He uses hand gesticulations to emphasise his words but the description of these gestures is too difficult to put into words.

LILONG LI is a very old and wise man with a gentle energy and is softly spoken. He has a very loving energy. He gives the impression of an ancient Tibetan monk. He uses gentle hand gesticulations to emphasise his words.

SHISHILA brings a very gentle, feminine energy and fills the room with her light, she is also known as the Lady of the Light and she speaks very softly. She also has a great love for humanity and wishes to help humanity. She uses hand and arm gesticulations to emphasise her words and when she leaves the room some of her gentle energy is left behind.

FATHER BARTHOLOMEW who spent his lifetime as a priest or monk when abortion clearly was a sin in the eyes of the Church gives a wonderful and enlightening talk on abortion and the contract a mother makes with her baby in these circumstances. He is a gentle man with a strong character who speaks from the heart and shows us how he has changed his very religious views about everything.

BAAL SHEM TOV comes in with a strong, powerful energy. He spent his life in the mystical traditions as a teacher and he speaks of the ancient mystery schools and brings forth this 'magic' some of which has been long forgotten. He also spent his life in the Jewish traditions but these traditions blend in with all other ancient traditions such as Chinese, Egyptian etc.

WINSTON WHITEHORSE has a strong, forthright energy and although he was a scribe in his time on earth he uses his words in a way that we can understand. He was a well educated man and his explanation on karmic energies between nations is given to us simply and succinctly.

KUKUWANA brings in a gentle, feminine energy and is softly spoken and she speaks of the earth and the elementals and her culture. She was a North American Indian and brings forth the wisdom of this culture which was about caring for the earth and everything that was a part of the earth.

1 - PAUL — July 3 2008

*...the great cosmic shift in perception, the shift
of reality, the shift that is occurring within your
planet, this shift is happening not just your on
physical plane but also on your spiritual plane...*

 For the first time that we come through we have to adjust our frequencies to this medium – greetings friends. We are aware that you wish to speak with us this afternoon and so first of all we would like to introduce ourselves.

*Carol had taken a little time to adjust to this
presence and her facial expression had changed to
almost resemble Paul features as in his picture in the
front of the book.*

We are from another place and time, we are from another galaxy, we are not what you call alien as we have had many incarnations within the earth but we also radiate out into the greater Cosmos as of most of the spiritual realms. We will introduce ourselves and we will give ourselves a name, we would like to give ourselves a name, the name of Red Cloud, we find this is very much on the ancient and indigenous tribes for this was one of our life times when we were known as Red Cloud. When we were in this incarnation and we liked this incarnation

1

as we were shamans and we were healers and medicine men of our tribe. There are more than one of us under the name of Red Cloud and you will meet each aspect of our personalities as our time continues and as we grow.

The information that we would bring forth to you today, we would like to talk to you about the great cosmic shift in perception, the shift of reality, the shift that is occurring within your planet, this shift is happening not just on your physical plane but also on your spiritual plane as the two begin to meet, merge and harmonise as one.

The ages that have gone and there are many ages that we have had on this earth plane, you do not know of them all but we will also give you that there was the age of weather patterns that changed the whole frequency of your planet before you wrote down, before you measured time, before you had history. The weather patterns were very different than what they are today and the earth was far more wet and the earth was much like a sea and this sea spread over vast areas, more so than the areas that you are aware of today for as the atmosphere dried out then the atmosphere changed and the Sun became far more accessible within your planet and changed and brought more life onto the planet.

However, you only call your physical manifestation on earth <u>life</u>, but there was life on this planet before your conscious awareness of life and we were at the earth and within the earth at this time, preceding your time, this is when the earth's foundation and core was being truly laid down. We have transcended time and space and bring through all of the different ages, we have seen the earth move and the changes become more and more productive to life. We would like to think of this as you spin up a penny and as you see the penny spinning around and around and as the penny speeds up, think of the earth that has been doing this over a great many eons and the energy that is placed around the earth and the build up of magnetic charge is what actually created the conditions on earth for your life forms to take place, however, do not believe that you are the only life forms that have ever inhabited your earth for when it was in this place of very fast spinning, the energy that was within the planet at that time was of a far finer frequency as it is more electric in its nature. This electric charge is what was finally brought through into the plants that were placed down as the earth slowed its rotation, this rotation slowed to the point where the atmosphere was born but the other planets that were around the cosmos of the earth, the making of the earth, were also spinning on a far quicker frequency and so do not think of just the earth as rotating faster, think of all your Universe, your Milky Way, your Galaxy as speeding up in vibration and then slowing down to support life - this had to happen and this is before time.

We are the overlords, we do not like to call ourselves the overlords but this is what you would understand us to be, the carers of your particular Galaxy, we did serve as the ancient traditions, we did serve in the mountains and we did serve in the prairies. We did come to the earth and bring our knowledge, we did not always remember who we were while we were on that earth plane at that time but have since had access to full knowledge of that incarnation.

We have seen much disruption, much disharmony, we have seen so much heartache that you perpetrate on the other, we have been a party to this and we have also had this done upon us. It is part of your evolution and yet we say to you it is time to stop, you have reached the point where you can no longer sustain this – it must stop. If it does not stop, you are heading for a fast tracking where there is destruction afoot but we say to you that there is an alternative possibility and this alternative possibility is children of the new generation but you who are inhabiting the earth today are those star children for your time will come when you will leave this earth and when you do join the earth again it will be as the star children of the new generation – that is recycling.

We thank you very much for allowing us this opportunity to share just a small portion of the knowledge that you have access to within yourself but for this time we will place the words in the air for your ears to rehear and reabsorb and open the new levels that are being awakened within you.

We thank you from the bottom of our hearts we would say for this opportunity and we bless you and we hope that we will meet again – we know that we will.

> *Carol returned to conscious reality rubbed her eyes and then stretched as if awakening from a deep sleep. The three of us sat quietly with broad smiles as the realisation of what had just happened began to dawn into our consciousness and also that we were at the beginning of a great adventure.*

> *(See Questions and Answers)*

2 - PAUL - July 18, 2008

*...what it is that you can do to change the earth
and it was asked if there is anything we can do
individually while on the earth plane.*

 Your thoughts on DNA are very interesting tonight, our thoughts on DNA are just a little bit of a variation, however we do believe you have access to a higher level of intuition, it is always available to you dear lady *(Alice)* - do you understand that? You are always able to ascend higher into those higher realms, it is not separate from you, it is just that there are very few moments when you access that transition and there is no separateness. That is when you get a little bit of an insight into what it is that you normally do not pay attention to but we can assure that it is always available for you at any time; it is just that you are more receptive to it in this moment.

> *There were several people gathered at a Spiritual Discussion evening and we had been talking about DNA and earth changes. Carol suddenly offered to do a trance session and when Paul came through it was obvious that he had been present and listening to our discussions. It would seem that he had impressed Carol that he would like to add to the*

discussion, and so the trance session.

You were talking about body structures, you have been speaking about what it is that you can do to change the earth and it was asked if there is anything we can do individually while on the earth plane. There are many things that you can do while on the earth plane, just the power of you being on the earth plane brings change to the world, every single thing that has ever been thought or it has been breathed life into, everything that has ever been placed forward in the earth is still existing, everything that you are experiencing in this moment and every dream that you will ever have in the future is in existence, all is in existence and all are working together. There is merely a choice - what is it that you wish to seek, do you wish to see disaster, pain, heartache, and do you wish to see how it does not work? If you choose to see that possibility then that is a possibility that you create in that instant of that which you seek, however if you choose to look at that and change the view and believe that it is absolutely perfect and absolutely healed and there is nothing out of place, in that instant you have made a different choice - that choice is that reality that you will experience.

You spend most of your time in the belief structures of that which has always been, you spend most of your time being what you are comfortable with, if you can stretch the boundaries and if you can allow those boundaries to take a different turn and to view things from a very different place then you can change the outcome. It does not take time, it does not take a long time, it can happen in seconds - now you are talking about healing, the whole of this is about healing for if you can do this in one instant of your life where you can take control of your choices and your thoughts and your beliefs, you can choose a different outcome, then you can change the whole structure of your biology.

So do you have a different strand of DNA, do you have a new strand of DNA, you are full and complete, you have always been full and complete. Every strand of DNA that is in your biology today has been with you for the whole of your existence in your physical incarnation, however have those switches been switched on? Have you been able to access that? Possibly not, there have been some who have come onto the earth who have those elements alive and active - you have called them Avatars, Masters, Healers, Alchemists, Wizard, Magician - all who can manoeuvre time and all who can manoeuvre space and outcome but it is available to you as your Masters have always taught you. There is nothing that is not available to you; it is just that you do not believe that you have the possibility to attain that.

Look at how you view the Master Christ, Christ was a human being in a physical form however he remembered who he was, he knew the power he held within him, he knew of his different chemistry, biology, he knew how to see you as completely whole and healthy so he knew that he could change anything with your physical experiences by viewing you as the opposite to how you saw yourself. So he saw you as whole and complete and in that instant he had the power within him to change the whole outcome of how you were feeling on the earth plane, base resonance comes into play here, you all have access to this - this is something that has been available to mankind.

You are archetypal, your mythic tales, are all telling your stories, about your own power but you tend to view them as outside of yourself, you are connected to every part of that and if you understand that then you can tap into any of those and you can activate them in your system and you can then have that access power run through your interior - you will be able to change the whole structure of your body. An enlightened being is merely someone who has access to a higher level of power, you get this in those moments when you spoke about getting those intuitive hits, getting those intuitive moments when you go into that place of knowing, you have merely bypassed your mind, you have merely bypassed that tool that gives you that rhyme, logic and reason, this is your belief structure, your whole belief structure has programmed and wired your brain. As you change the belief structures you change the wiring within the brain, this changes the chemicals that fire throughout that beautiful jelly-like substance. Electro-magnetics that is what pumps through the body, which is what pumps through the brain, that is what gives you the sickness and carries the pulses through to your consciousness and so you go out and live that consciousness every day of your life.

The children who are being born into the earth we say and we have heard that they are now called indigo children, are they true indigo children or are they children who are being born into a new time of consciousness - do they understand their own power? We would say that they no longer follow the tribal influences but are coming in to shake them up and to ask questions and to say no, these are the indigo children, these are the children of the new millennium, these are the children who will carry your future generations forward. You have access to this at any time, you have access to everything, there has never been anything that you could not access, the only thing that has stopped you from accessing is your own limitations and belief structures and as you believe in limitation and believe that you can not, if that resonates within you at any level then you have stopped the growth forward and you can no longer access that because the outcome to that belief is a change experience.

So look at what you believe and listen to how you speak for as you speak so shall you create, the power of the word that is spoken resonates from that wave, that impulse of limitation and then you speak it and the breath is the power of creation. You are changing, you are truly changing and the whole earth that you inhabit is changing but it is meant to change, as you come to a close of a cycle, you have to change in order for the new cycle to meet and move you forward - this is the whole process of change. As the world changes, the single person who stands with a new revelation is still part of the whole yet they are somehow separate and individual as part of that whole consciousness, they are that new flame that spirals and moves forward, that grows, your consciousness is changing, your earth is changing.

Your earth is changing because you will give up the need for your ego, the need to be right, the need to know best, that need to be sanctified, honoured. I have heard it said once, which made me laugh, that I just needed that pat on the back because then I have been acknowledged for the deed that I have done - then we go back to the Masters, did they want that pat on the back, did they wanted to be acknowledged. You will go into a time of humility; you will lose the ego, now this is truly the indigo child in its magnificent crystalline form, when you give up the need for yourself, when you understand humility, when you understand the need to be totally insignificant.

There was a great Master called Francis of Assisi, now Francis of Assisi was born with much money and he gave away the money and the robes of his father and he built a new church but that church was symbolic of the church within his own temple, this is the New Age where you give away your externals and you bring them home to the internal temple and you give of yourself. Could you on any level walk up to somebody who has a major deformed body, could you hold that person in your arms and see love, could you see them whole, complete and perfect and could you find compassion in your heart, could you give them the clothes off your back? - this is the New Age, the age where the ego is no longer the driving force within your life - the ego must go and this is the shift of the ages.

To our dear friend this is the end of time, the end of time and new millennium, the ninth centre. We have a Vedic[1], we have had a whole structure of power that you have understood the eighth centre but we are now giving you the new structure which is the ninth centre of reality, from the ninth dimension of creation. This

---

1. Vedic – the language of the Vedas – an older form of Sanskrit.

is not going to happen externally, it is happening to you internally, it can only happen internally so when the world becomes filled with chaos, pain, when you see wrongdoing, do not put more wrongdoing into that moment but look at it and give thanks that you experienced it, love it for what it is and let it go for what it has been, take the wisdom from it and walk forward with it for that is who you are now.

Looking into your future will not help you, looking into your past cannot finance you, living in the future and the past in this moment of creation, now that is your power and who does not have access to that power. You have no idea what gods you are, the God is not external, the God is internal, the God is love, compassion, mercy, humility, and these are the new powers, the new power stations of the new millennium.

Now consciousness and beliefs are bred into your very being, your heart and your body's rhythm that is your connection to that magnetic force that lives within the Universe - this pulsation is what you are wired to. When the magnetics of your earth change and the polarities breathe a different frequency through your heart and pulse through the entrainment of a new vibrational frequency - now you have access to a higher and finer level of power and you truly become creators. That magnetic shift is that glue that sticky substance that you have called belief that is what creates what you see in your external world, that is the essence of time and how long you will have to take that time to change and create anything.

If you change the magnetics of your body and you live the frequency, now the glue is not set with such density and you can change, you can change your beliefs in an instant and it is not linear time and you wonder why you have so many illnesses and deaths on your planet, because the glue of belief is what creates the tumours within your body, your life that you have experienced, that is the tumours, the blockages, the viruses that live within your blood. Remember the pulse of your body in the heart and the heart pulsates the blood which is the fluidity and movement of life.

We thank you for receiving us this evening, it is our honour and pleasure to be allowed to speak with you this evening and we shall now take our leave, thank you.

3 - PAUL - JULY 24 2008

...your spirit, about who you are.

 Friends – just adjusting the instrument to receive the energy – it is easier this week as she has been working already this day.

There are many subjects that we could come and speak to you about but today we are of a mind to speak to you about your spirit, about who you are. We would like to open up some doors for you in the recognition of why it is you would come in to have this physical experience. The last time we met, friends, we spoke to you about being within the earth elements before the earth really began, we spoke to you about being formless, formless in essence, this essence is who you are but this does not mean too much to you for you do not know or recognise this time do you? So we would like to try and make it a little bit clearer for you.

Your Bible does state quite a bit of information about it, however, it is not truly representative of what you are – you are the God force but it does not tell you what that God force is. We would endeavour through your language to try and share what this God force is for it is not what you think it is as we are not what you think we are – it is particles, vibration and sound, sound which is related to light, in fact we would like to share this concept with you – that you are light, every aspect of you is light and how can this be?

When you look at the Sun you see the mass of the Sun, the yellow sphere, that sphere that you recognise in your orbit, however, you do not all see the rays that are emitted from the Sun, the essence of the Sun, you are very much like this. Think of your Sun as the Creator and think of yourself as the light that is sent forth, it is in essence the heat, the vapour of that mass but God is not a mass, God is the Universe, the Universe is the mass, the Universe appears like air to you with these little blobs of matter that have accumulated, grown and are now supporting life on the different spheres. This essence and heat, this evaporation – have you ever thought of yourself as evaporation from the God force, an evaporation energy mass, a mist, this is what you are, you are merely a mist, a misty milk mist that pulls together in a particular pattern from the very centre of your heart.

The Universe is bigger than you could ever imagine, it is expansive and it is continually expanding as it grows it envelops more space, space is empty so it is infinitive, it is infinitesimally big, it is inconceivable that you would never be able to really grasp just how large your Universe is, you are not even a pinprick in your understanding, your entire Galaxy is not even a pinprick. We would liken it to one receptor in your brain and the brain being the Universe for your brain is a representative of the universal energy – this was very necessary to bring consciousness and the consciousness that lives within your brain is that vibration and that essence of the pulse and force. As this energy manifests from, let us say we must use an analogy for you to comprehend, so we have the Universe, we have your Galaxy, we have your Sun, we have the Light, that heat of the Sun, we have the planet that sustains you with this breath, this essence, and we have your brain which is the consciousness of that essence, we have the heart which is the essence of your earth and all are interconnected. When you say that you are one, you are truly one for every person has one element of the Divine that is their spark, it is merely their representative pattern, the pattern is the individual, the pattern is what makes you self but the pattern is just another manifestation that you give breath and life to through the force of the brain. The electrical, Magnetical pulse vibrates to the electrical, Magnetical pulse of your Sun of the Universe of the Galaxy. Think of the consciousness God force as your thought patterns, you do not see the thought patterns yet you recognise them.

Every particle is made up of that thought pattern when you see this in the brain, the brain is made up of many spheres, and there are many parts of the brain that work together to give you a unified consciousness. From this unified consciousness you then have the antenna that the consciousness, that impulse is connected to, that impulse then goes down the rod, the rod then sends that information to the relevant parts for you to individually express – you know this as your thoughts and personality, your behavioural quirks. This pulse is what regulates your heart; the heart is the pulse that keeps that current fluid through your body.

The collective spirit is that individual pattern of light that is emitted like the rays of your Sun, the rays of your Sun filter down like, you might call it stardust sprinkling the earth, and it is you who are the sprinkles of this dust, cosmic light, cosmic vibration, and cosmic pattern. You see it as solid, you see yourself as solid, however this dust is merely magnetically charged and like dust on a surface it is attracted to each other to make balls of dust, you do not see the individual dust particle but when they are mass that are being electrically charged and drawn together you get the physical manifestation of the building up of the blocks of that dust particle. That is what you are and yet the dust particle is not solid it is millions of this particle and it all comes together like the ball of wool, as it unravels, it unravels to a solid mass of vibrational pattern, the vibration pattern is then sent into the earth and you recognise each other, like you would recognise the end of the string and where the string will go if it is unravelled it would fall to the floor for it now has weight. Until this happens, you are weightless, this is the point that transcends from holographic to physical manifestation and yet we could un-charge, we could set the polar opposite in you and we could send, instead of implosion, together we could send explosion apart, this explosion apart would be the individuation of each of the particles bringing you back to dust, the original dust particle. It is no mistake that you say ashes to ashes and dust to dust for you are that, it is merely symbolic of a vague memory a very external memory that you have contained within your circuitry.

You are electrically charged beings, the electricity is the life force, you are like the bee buzzing around and we laugh when we see you busy, busy, busy, you buzz from here, you buzz from there, you are very caught up. There is one part of you that is manifested; ninety-nine percent of you remain this stream. If you think of spirit as I come through this very day, this light beam that is my individual packet of energy, my individual vibrational pattern, it is blending with the vehicle's pattern and I am taking charge of that conscious expression.

The other vibration that keeps this vehicle alive is still present but it has been very gently removed back and my presence, my ball of dust has more density to it than hers at this moment as I work through her, but if you view me and her, you would see two beams of light as it extends in time, it extends back in time, it is a highway to the point, to the centre of the Universe, all physical manifestations, all individual manifestations lead back to this infinitesimally small point which is the Universe and yet in paradox I have said that the Universe is infinitesimally large – how can this be? Because the universal charges, I believe you call this the North Pole, the polarisations, the opposites – we must now go into opposition.

The opposite's attraction – it pulls away so although your source goes back to the infinitesimally small point of the original mass, that mass is then borne into space and it is expansive and absolute in its nature. When you work to develop this ability, when you work to recognise yourself, who you are, when you become aware of the pulsating of who you are, you are merely tapping into that stream. How far back you follow that stream will determine the information pull that you can access, you have to have the physical point of attraction on the earth or there would be no point in the Universe existing at all for you.

So you live your lives in this paradox where you view the world as large, solid, real and time, however, this source is infinitesimally small and has no weight and has no time – this is what is meant when we say it is the space between each bar of sound, it is the space between the musical notes, it is the space between the solid and the eternal – this is the spirit, this is the universal principle, this is who you are, it is the silence between the words, this is the essence of who you are and you do not see the silence yet it is the silence that makes the speech recognisable or it would become just a burble to you and unintelligible. This is who you are – we are happy to bring this information but we feel that our language, even this makes it impossible to truly open you to who you are but we are in polar opposites, we are in the extremes, when you perceive the largeness of the Universe, please know that it is the smallest point in the tapestry.

Before we go we would like to speak to you of healing for this is a part of your being that is very relevant to your time and point in history. The healing vibration has been given to you, the consciousness of the self and the self-healing is being given to you at this point in time because up until this point through the eons and development of who you are, you never truly understood that you were the problem in the first place and how you perceive that problem was the very part that stopped you from healing. As you heal, as you heal the planet, you will heal yourself. As you heal the planet, as you heal self, you will move into this higher vibration, you will come back and you will wake up and you will tap in to that stream and that will be the finalising for the earth plane in this dimension and point in time.

What will then happen will be that your earth will change, the earth and its structure and it will become lighter and more finite and you will be a far more resolute point of time and you will be able to heal and you will transcend into timelessness. You think it will be going back to spirit but it will not be – there will be a time on this plane which you will not see where you will not be restricted by physical gravity, you will transcend this limitation and you will be able to transport yourself in no time, the cosmic glue will shift and the cosmic glue is consciousness – that is what you are working towards – that is what the Masters have always come to teach you. You had to go through evolving doors, through the spirals of time to get to that point and when you do hold your hand out and to manifest an object, a crystal, a flower, a star for that is the true Master. When we said that you were learning mastery that is what you are learning, that is the true meaning of your spiritual growth, which is the true meaning of your life on this earth, which is what that cosmic sleep is about as you awaken.

The part that is awakening is that part that is healing.

We thank you.

4 - PAUL – July 31, 2008

...speak about your healing and about healing the
body, healing the mind and healing your spirit...

 Greetings friends, we are very pleased to be here this day so that we may speak with you. We have been waiting and speaking to the medium since this morning when she was lying ready to wake, we told her we would like to speak today about your healing and about healing the body, healing the mind and healing your spirit.

We wish to bring in some information along those lines if we may please. As you know, healing is a very personal thing for you to experience, no two people will ever experience the vibration exactly the same -   you are able to access the level of healing that you yourself can manage.

We will talk about those who are very plugged in, plugged in would be the word, their circuit board runs toward the global consciousness and they are very power structured, they only believe in that which comes from the force behind them, they never really understand that the power of healing comes from within them. If they could understand that the power shift will change from them and the external, then they will, I am sure, start the healing trend on your earth plane, your healing trends are already changing. As a matter of fact you have already started to change the program from this external power behind you to the external power in front of you – what do we mean by saying that? The power behind you is the power of your own consciousness, it is that conscious thought, that conscious pattern that you invest your circuit board into, they are as much behind you for you do not see them clearly.

Healing comes from that place of magnetic attraction, it comes from the vibration of wishing to be well and though we are very aware at this time on your earth plane there are a great many who do not wish to be well, they find themselves being very plugged into being unwell - the un-wellness of their soul matches the un-wellness of the planet. Your planet is struggling to stay well, your planet is struggling to breathe, your planet is struggling to stay pure, your planet is struggling to stay clear, it is all condensed into a matter, a particle of dust, it is not clear, it does not cleanse itself.

Therefore the energy vibration of healing feels like a cloud of dust around you – how do you get the clarity in that dust? How do you take the clarity from that dust? This is not done easily for this takes a change of monumental proportion, you have set up the power in front of you, you have set up people as being the ones who will give you the healing, you have set up the external power base that you will get that healing given to you and you will not do anything, you will merely show up and that healing will be given to you. We will turn that around, we will say that unless you choose to do the healing, you will never truly receive any healing vibration – you will be receiving therapy, only therapy.

Your skies and your planet are a reflection of your global health – do you think that you are healthy as an individual or do you think that you are healthy as a global mass? Your global mass is what brings health, when the global mass come in on a vibration of being healthy, of being empowered, of being able to heal thyself, then that healing energy will clear, it will crystallise, you are crystal in nature, your vibrations are crystalline. When you are living in this fog, the vibrational pull to you is taken a level of degrees, it is taken down an octave, this octave is the difference between dis-ease or health, the dis-ease lodges itself in the dust particles in the cell tissue, this you have known as your cancerous tumours, they are dead, they are the dead weight of your life and they sit in the cell tissue. You have to be able to access that crystalline vibration, you have to be able to lift up your vibrational pull to a far clearer reception, with this reception, think of photosynthesis, think of that vibrational imprint that you pull to you as a resource from the external global orb, from the God Source – this is that light that you bring into your body. The photosynthesis burns away the manifestation, the weight of your life but this does not help in the healing process if you do not get to the core issue of why you have become unwell.

As you have become unwell, it has taken your whole life and the whole experience of your life to bring you to this point so you have to backtrack through the story of your life, as you backtrack through the story of your life; you take a look at yourself from a totally different perspective. You look at the events of your life – we would suggest that you become very detached from how you are perceived by others, this is probably one of the most important aspects of your healing – what do the other people in your life think of you, this is where you will find that dead weight because this is the program that you will run and this is the program that will read your life.

As you have been interacting with the people in your life, they have set up certain expectations on how they believe that you should behave and as you behave in that manner you give a lot of yourself over to that globe, to that consciousness of those other people. This is a more individual aspect of what it was we were trying to explain earlier about the global consciousness. Your globe sets down its set of standards, your globe sets down that you should have this life, that this should happen at this time, that you should do this type of thing, this is the way that your family will be, this is how you will live your life.

All over the globe you will find little mini imprints of this certain mind pattern, however as you go through your actual life, as you go into your individual life, you bring that manifestation down into personal life belief patterns. Belief patterns are the patterns that are governing your very existence, this belief pattern is the pattern that you have moulded your entire existence around, if you wish to see how you will become well, then you go into that belief pattern, you look at the expectations that you have placed on yourself in accordance to the people in your life, whether those people be the tribal structure of your family or the community structure of your life.

As you become aware of this in your own cell tissues, you begin to feel the sense of the weight that in clarity, that global dust, that fog that placed itself in that beautiful segment of your body, into the organs, into the very biology of who you are – this program is like a blueprint as it is in your very fabric, it is in the tapestry, it is a woven colour on the fabric that makes the blanket, that blanket is a colour because of its individual strand – this is how your molecular structure is set up. The molecular structure then runs the belief pattern; it is the belief pattern that brings the illness or the wellness into the body so how do you start to unplug from the belief of others?

We would suggest that there are three main ways that you can do this. First of all you must believe in your own wellbeing, first of all you must see yourself everyday as very healthy, very strong and very fit. You must run a new program, you must not tell yourself that you cannot achieve all that you have set out to achieve; you cannot tell yourself that you are tired, you cannot tell yourself that you cannot do this, you cannot tell yourself any of the negative programs. We want to tell ourselves these negative programs because in the negative program this is the very essence that gives us permission to sit down and to do nothing, we do not need to put any expectation on our own being, we can just exist, we can just live the life frivolously, wasting the time that we have on the earth.

You will notice that happens with a great mass of the people, every time that they emerge and every time that they set down a goal in front of them they then start to run this negative program, we cannot do this, I will not do this, I will not do this because I do not understand where this will lead me which leads us to the second part.

We have to envision, we have to see the long term goal of what it is we are working to achieve, we have to have a direction, we have to set a map, the map is the compass of your being, the map is the radar that you will be guided to, you place a map in front of you, you then follow and you have the direction set and you then take on all that comes to you so that you may move forward and march through time, time is the illusion and you transcend the limitations of time and you do this by becoming engrossed in what it is you have set as the objective to do. So you run the program of what it is that you can do, you change your belief pattern into that which you must do and that you can do, that you have the energy, that you have the ability, that you have all of the tools that you need, then you set the direction, the radar, the compass and you set the outcome, you make it manageable, you move it forward and time transcends. Time moves forward constantly, time speeds up, the more passionate you become about this time, the more passionate you become in your life, the more time speeds up until you reach the goal of where you want it to be. This is where step three is then placed in action.

You will then set your radar on the next level of your being, this is where you take it back internally, this is where you turn the radar around, this where you go back into gratitude for all of life that has supported you to this point, this is where you take that compass and you place it within you – now you will be ready to bring this that you have done and you have achieved out to the masses. This is where you will be guided to take this that you have mastered into the other people who are in your life; this is what we are talking about as mastery of your soul.

When you become a master being, you become a being of

Light, the Masters are in total control of their external world and their internal world, they are in total control of where they have set the radar of what they wish to achieve in this world and then from that point they put the focus on that perhaps to reach that point. As they do this, they then bring it back into the world and they are now born of the world, this is how this practice goes. You can do this with the healing – if you have mass building up of this grey matter, of this weight, that has been born of the blueprint of the negative program, I cannot do this, and the expectations that others have placed in myself that I cannot do, then you will turn it around. You will look inside the grey matter and you start to change the program, you will look at the people who you have put the beliefs into and you will then step back, you will then change that focus and that direction.

There are a lot of people on your earth who truly wish to help all of the people all of the time, you cannot do this for then you are placing your expectations on other people and this is then collecting the cosmic dust, the grey matter in their cell tissue – this is how this illness in this body will start to manifest. What is it that it takes for you to start to look and change the program, what is it that it takes; it takes you to actually come to that point where you are faced with not being able to stay on the earth, as you are faced with this, and you are faced with your mortality. As you are faced with your mortality then you will take that power from those external people and you no longer care what it is that they expect of you, now you are telling them "I am in a journey for my life" and I don't particularly care what you want from me for now it has to be my centre focus. If you do not make that shift and you continue to try to meet everybody else's expectations of what they have placed on you into manifestation then you will ultimately lose the battle for your life – this is part of the healing process.

We are talking about the molecular structure, the magnetics that you create in your life, we are talking about the tapestry of your life, your feelings are from the mental field, your feelings of who you are come from a force far greater than you – you plug into the global consciousness, you plug into the universal forces, this is who you are – these are the people that you are. Once you recognise yourself for that you will then understand that **you have three fears**, three fears that are completely governed and running your life, as you recognise these fears, you will start to use these three steps that I have given you and you will start to work with them on the healing vibration.

The **first fear** is that you will come in on the understanding that you are **totally and utterly abandoned,** you will always feel that you are abandoned, as you feel that you are abandoned, this is part of that grey matter that sits in your fibre, in your tapestry, this is part of that universal fear based program that is running and ignited and alive in your cell structure. The **other universal fear** that you will face is that of **being alone**, there is a difference between being abandoned and being alone, abandonment makes you feel that you have lost those who you love, it grieves your inner stomach, it gives that part of your body anxiety, it puts you on the fight or flight mode. This fear of abandonment makes you cling to all of the other people and resources in your life and you will take a lot of the emotional baggage that they bring to you. The **second fear** of abandonment, of being alone, is the fear that **you will never be good enough** for those who around you, that you will always be left and you cannot care for yourself.

The **other one** that you will encounter along the way **will be the fear of needing approval**, this fear of approval will come in under the banner of always seeking to place yourself in other people's hands, of always running your self worth through their expectations of you, this is a manifestation of global consciousness. If you were a girl, if you were born and you had your program running which your society told you that you cannot be a woman and be clever, you are a woman, you are stupid, then you will run that approval through everybody else and it will set your sense of self.

All three of these really live in that part of your being, they are all governed by that fight or flight, and they sit in the intuitive part of your biology in the molecular structure. All of the illnesses that you will face upon this earth will be in a part of that, it will be an expression of that tapestry that you have woven, as you work through these fears, you will work through the fears from eon to eon, you will work with them over and over again, you will work through them on many levels, you will bring them from the most disempowered part of your being and you will take them through the door into the most empowered part of your being. When you have brought them through that empowered part of your being you will then become the master of your being for in that instant this is where you truly find power because the people in your life no longer hold that kind of authority in your being.

If you are left alone, then that is fine, you cannot be alone, you know this now because you no longer live that program. If you feel abandoned, you know that you cannot be abandoned, so you can allow those people to leave your life and you can do it without losing yourself. If you need to feel approved of by other people you understand that you are giving yourself over to that person and behaving the way they wish you to behave. You know that this is not acceptable so you will not allow that part of your being to leave that part of your body and so therefore you will bring your tentacles back in – the clarity that you get with this is very important to understand in the creation of the healthy carbon unit, you will only ever get ill as you work through these three fears, how you work through them are as many and as varied and as possible an experience on the earth but you are in the process of becoming the masters of your being.

When you come into spirit at the end of an incarnation, where will you find yourself? Will you find yourself in that place where you have left the earth? Will you find yourself at dis-ease and discord with your body? This is a question that must be answered in accordance to the mirror side of this for if you have not mastered this on the earth plane and have passed by illness in particular, then you will find yourself as you awaken on the other side with that program still running – this is the incarnational process. You will not be able to be unwell, you will still hold that belief pattern, that pattern that has created the physical being will still be ignited in that spiritual essence, you will have the all, the whole, the entirety to base this experience on but that individual spark of the part that was created that has come back to the spiritual soul will still hold that blueprint within its very tapestry. This is where you will incarnate again and so the cycle will continue, it will continue for the entirety until you get the program.

Your heart is an indication of all of the events in your life, when you incarnate into the earth plane, your heart is the barometer of how well you have lived your life, it is the barometer of how you have coped with these experiences, it is the barometer of what you have displayed to each other and what you have put into creation on the earth, this is why the heart becomes sick if it has been putting out a very negative program based on those three principles that we have spoken of – that is the magnetic pulse that is tapped into the core of your earth, that is the frequency that comes off the earth, this is the point where you will set up the experiences in your life, this is the point of attraction, this is the magnetic pull back into the earth, this is the ozone of your body. You understand the ozone of the earth, you have an ozone layer, you have a layer that is keeping in all of the earth vibrations and keeping out all of the heat vibration, this is the crust of the body, this is the heart, this is the pulse that is emitted when the heart gets sick, when the heart is not pumping the love, the heart fades out as your ozone has faded out, it gets holes in its being. It is very, very important that you understand that you will not feel the beat of this drum in your external field yet the beat of this drum is very much a part of the external field, this is what you will experience and what you will draw to you, please understand this part with your biology – it is an absolute machine, you are a meat machine, make no doubt about it and how you live your life in the emotions, the emotions are the blueprint, the emotion that you feel you emit from this point of your being which is the heart point.

This is that blueprint that is now being put into manifestation, mind and body are not of the same substance and yet mind and body are intricately woven as the same substance – this is a paradox of the Universe that wherever you will find two units working side by side they will be as intricately patterned as you would imagine, it is possible they will be interwoven, they will be layered upon layer within each other, they will be dependent on each other and yet they will still be a separate part of each other, they will never fully be one and the same – this is the mind, spirit and body connection. The mind is your spirit, it is not a separate force, the spirit is that part of you that is eternal, it is that part of you that is light, light governs your entire body, and light governs your entire being.

When your spirit is connected to your body what you are effectively doing is that you are turning down the light as you would see it being turned on one of your dimmers, it merely goes from high and as it goes down the chain it becomes dimmer and dimmer. The carbon unit is that part of you where you would put the light switch off, the two are not the same and yet they are made up of the same. When the pattern of the mind meets the body that is what it turns into, emotional experience and from the emotional experience it uses the external world as its information pool, it is a matrix in its very definition. If you were to see it through your spirit eyes when you place your hand into the air it would be the same as placing your hand into the water, as you move your hand across the water, the water moves and you will see ripples, your matrix and your belief patterns are of the same and as you move your hand through it, as you work through it from the heart as you send the experience from the mind into the body, into experience and send it into the earth, it is almost like that ripple that moves as a hand through the water.

This is the Divine Matrix that you are made up of, this is the essence of who you are, and the external world is truly the essence of your internal world. When we say this we say this with this consciousness that if you an angry human being, you will only attract those who live in an angry world, that angry world will live next to you, through you and be a part of your experience, however, if you move to the house next door and the person who is living in the house next door and they place their hands in the water, they are looking through the water of peace, the matrix of peace, they will only draw to them those who vibrate peace. So their experience of that pool of water, of that matrix, will be a peaceful matrix, so you can have two people standing side by side, living side by side but at the same time you can have two totally independent universes being created from the source – the source is the heart, the heart then like the waves goes out and filters into that global consciousness, that is the individual aspect of that. The more global aspect of that is the offshoot from that, this is the part where the whole is woven into consciousness, this is the part that is the full picture of who you are, this is everything that has ever lived, everything that has ever been thought, this is literally the global bin, this is the bin that you would place your beliefs and rubbish in, this is the bin of the Universe, this is how you have treated your earth and your consciousness.

As you start to realise that if you place rubbish in the bin, the bin stinks so when you start to become aware that the experience around you in the whole of the globe, in the whole of the earth is the bin where you place all of the beliefs then you start to change your beliefs and the whole thing changes to mirror that belief but it is still a ripple in time for it cannot erase all that has been lived, all that has been thought, all that has been experienced by every single person. It is the collectiveness of all of that individual vibration of thought and emotion that you have been pulsating throughout the earth, it is the conglomerate of the whole, we are using our hands to help you understand that this is part of the whole and that you are a simple little sparkle in that whole.

When you move from anger into peace, the emotion that you express is far stronger. Remember we said that the spirit is of the highest light bulb, that the physical body is of the lowest light bulb and as you pull your vibration up to the highest light you bring that light into your whole body, your whole carbon unit becomes more vibrant, it vibrates more life, it vibrates more light, it vibrates more love, it vibrates this peace. This peace is then sent out further in that matrix and that peace then changes and becomes stronger in that global consciousness, you cannot affect the other people who choose to stay in anger, who choose to stay in the lower levels, they are not ready to vibrationally match you, they must stay on the lower frequency.

You have come to understand the lower frequencies as the devil, as evil, it is not evil, it is merely a state of maturation, they will get to this point, however they have the choice of what they choose to put into their experience. If they continue, you can stand by them, you can send them love, you can project peace but it will be like an arrow that just gets delivered back out into the Universe, however this is not wasted, this goes out to the mass of the earth, this goes out into that crust that we were speaking of and it holds it in, it keeps it in and slowly over time in your linear experience, it builds peace. These people will incarnate again and again and they will slowly plug into that source, remember we said that they can never lose any aspect of the creation, everything that has ever been experienced will still be in a manifested state on some level so when they are ready to vibrationally match that love that you are projecting to them they will then pick up that vibration and it may be that little dust, that little stardust, that little light that changes.

This may sit in vibration, this may sit in escrow, this may sit in monumental states of static being for eons, this may sit for generations, this may then be tapped into and brought to them, you are thinking with linear, with physical, with limitations. We are asking you to open and to expand the entirety of your understanding in the Universe for everything that you have ever experienced will still remain in 100 years and you yourself can access that which you have today in that incarnation, if you choose to in 100 years from now.

We wish to tell you who has brought this today, we have called ourselves the consciousness of the Red Cloud, they allowed that lady to see who this was so that we could project a face onto our work but we really chose a pattern of a life that we lived on the earth in order to give you the visual but we truly do not and will not ever look like a human being but as long as you are happy with the appearance we chose to present, we would be happy for you to call us Paul.

We will take our leave now, thank you.

5 - Shishila, Lady of the Light – August 14, 2008

*…what happens when you make the transition
from your life to the veil of the afterlife…?*

 Health, your bodies, your lives, all that you see before you is that point of reality that you view the world through. Perceptions – we would like to talk to you today about perception. My name is Shishila, I am the Lady of the Light, I am the High Priestess – you were speaking of me last session and so I felt that it was time for me to make myself known to thee.

(As Shishila presented Carol's face softened and became radiant, and Mary and I knew immediately that we had a new entity as it was so different from how Paul presents.)

We would like to talk to you today about the dark side, the dark side and light side, about consciousness and about your journey within that conscious frame. We would like to speak to you about what happens when you make the transition from your life to the veil of the afterlife. The afterlife, that makes us laugh for it is the life before life, it is the life within life, it is the life after the life, there is no distinguishing for although you incarnate onto

31

the earth, there is still that part of you that is in the afterlife – but how can that be?

If you are incarnated in the earth and are alive then how can there be such a large aspect of you in the afterlife? This bears a lot of thought, it is because you never leave the afterlife, you are always living and contained within the afterlife, the before life and the experience of living - you will only recognise the different stages as you prepare for the incarnation. We spoke last time of the soul grouping, we spoke last time of how that soul grouping then incarnates and chooses the map, the blueprint of the life. We would like to now speak about when you have had that life, when you have lived that life and then you return back to the Source.

The life that you have lived on the earth plane will determine exactly where it is that you find yourself in the afterlife - where you have lived, how you have thought, what you have experienced but the most important part will be the intention and the action that have been lived and done to others within the context of that life, that sets up the vibration, the pull, that shuts down the magnetics of where it is that you would find yourself if you could change some intentions within your life - as you change your intentions, as you change your direction, as you change the pattern of your life and that pattern is the emotion.

We will talk to you about the emotion for you experience emotion on the earth plane and you measure it physically, your emotion is what comes with you when you leave the body. Your emotional state, your emotional vibration, your emotional feelings and output, that amplification that you have magnetically pulsated throughout your physical body into the external parts of your reality, this is what you take into the afterlife, this is what you take into the after death state. If you take in an emotion of darkness, if you take in the emotion of greed, of serving the self, of being selfish then where you find yourself will vibrationally match that emotion. Have you ever considered that death is merely the extension of emotion, there is only one way to live and be alive and that is through the emotion, the emotion is a product of the mental field, the mental field is a product of the emotion but the emotion is the idea, the perception placed into life through your emotion, through your heart – this is why the heart is such an important organ, this is why that pulse of your breath, of your heartbeat, of the rhythm of your life is what we call your point of manifestation.

So you have lived a life and you have lived it to serve yourself, you have lived it in greed, you have lived it in destruction, you have lived it with the intention to serve only your purpose, you have walked over who you need to walk over to achieve the goals that you have set for yourself, you have not given freely but you have taken but more importantly, when you have taken you have hoarded more than you could possibly need. Now you are of the earth plane when you are in this vibration, you are living and this entire life process that you have been living has slowly but surely been poisoning you, it poisons you every day, every minute, every second of your life. It poisons you from the inside to the outside and eventually your body says "I cannot stay healthy, I will have to push you out of this physical incarnation" and you will have to come home to repeat the process and to start to repair the healing that you have done.

Now you have come to the earth plane with this as your program, this is the journey, this is the intention so you view your behaviour as perhaps being bad but it is not for if you are living it, it serves its purpose.

So you have now left the physical world, you have now made the sojourn into the astral plane, you have called it the astral, that is not what we call it but you will be happy to continue with that word as you are comfortable there. We call it the steps of existence, we gave this to this person who is giving this information, and we gave this through the medium as a meditation to help you to open to our vibration but let us not be detracted from where we are going on this journey.

We have now gone through the passing, the sojourning into

the afterlife, this afterlife is of course merely an extension of your physical life so when you awaken and you have separated from that physical being you now, let us say, open your eyes. The eyes are the consciousness of your soul, you are now in the place that vibrationally matches the life that you have lived while on the earth – what is it that you find? Do you find yourself with a love of light, with a love of harmony, peace and happiness around you? Do you find yourself surrounded with loving, giving and celebrating the majesty of who you are? Do you believe that this is what you will find when you are on the other side? Most of you would say no, if I have lived a life where I have taken, where I have maimed, where I have hurt, where I have caused nothing but sorrow for others and have taken for myself then it would stand to your reason that you would be surrounded in hell.

This is the word that you have given us; we would suggest that this is not actually the transitional stage that you will find yourself in – if you can make that connection to the Light Source who will come to meet you. As you separate your consciousness, there is another part of your being that will remain in a semi-state, you have separated from the physical body and you have created a shell, this is an etheric shell which is a body double, a match without the organs, you are the meat machine, this is the colour vibration of you. This has to separate from the body and now between the three aspects of the soul, you will stand in this body of consciousness, while you are in this body of consciousness a higher soul will come to greet with you, they will spend that time and they will make you aware of their presence slowly. This is an integral part of your passing process for if you do not see that pinprick, that manifestation of pattern of light you might see it like a prism through the Sun hitting that prism energy through the crystal. This is what it will appear to you as you stand in this place, in this etheric double, in this essence vibrational body. The body will still be quite solid to you as you are now in the belief that you are still contained in the body, you may even wish to carry the characteristics of the body that you have just left.

If you get this energy, if you see this vibration as it meets with you, you will want, by its very definition and the feel of that love, to migrate towards it, you will be drawn like a magnet, you will be pulled to this vibrational colour and as you see this colour it becomes clearer. Over space and time your body disintegrates on the earth, your body starts to decay, as it starts to decay, the energetic pull is now weakening, it is now releasing that vibrational body further from the field, so if you were able to see it, it would look like a three-pronged effect, you would see the physical body, perhaps as you would put it in the coffin, you would see the physical body decaying and you would see the energetic body slowly, bit by bit, frame by frame, moving away from that pull, you would then see the energy body coming in to meet it.

Now is this energy, this vibration, the light colour you or is it another aspect of divinity? Well this is the question that you might ask yourself – we would say to you that it is you, it is your higher part coming to meet the middle level of your being as you are in this transcendental state. As this part of your soul becomes recognisable, it will take a form, it will take a form that you have to trust or to love or to have connection to, now this does not have to be a family member or somebody who you can recognise, this can be an essence or an angelic presence. This is where the mythology of the angels with the wings was born for if you expect to see an angel, you will see that part of yourself as an angel, now you have met yourself as you truly are, you are an introspective part of the self looking at the external part of that being but you are all one.

Now perhaps the physical body has been cremated or is now in the earth, now you are being drawn into a new part of your being, it will be like a mirror and this mirror will be made of different light frequencies. It will shimmer and it will appear to be solid in the beginning and as this energy starts to come closer to you and you to it, it will begin to look shimmery, it will begin to look transcendental, it will begin to look like a liquid substance and it will be more penetrable. On the other side of this, which is your soul, you will start to see a light; this light will be in the distance, this point, this little spark of light, this part is now waiting for you, it is like that whisper that calls to you, come, come, come to me as a small child runs to the mother's arms. As you move through this point of your soul's manifestation, as you move into you become more essence than the intermediary, the shell that you have been carrying, again with the physical death of the body, begins to disintegrate. As this disintegration takes place the body becomes more light filled, now you are at that point where it is a shell, an empty shell and it is almost like the egg that is cracked to release the yolk in the centre, that yolk is the aspect of the self, the white is that luminous field that you have been viewing externally as that rippling, mirrored effect.

You are now drawn into the very essence of this mirror, you are now drawn through that mirror and you are now in that state of cleansing, of clearing, the hard shell has been released, the black muck, the lower vibrational pull, the energy of the emotions that you have felt on the earth are now in essence being ripped and stripped from your very interior but it is not a painful experience, it is merely the experience of releasing. It is like when you have had a memory of something that has really caused you worry and at the end of that worry the answer now stands before you and you are now in excitement that you are going to meet the essence of what it was you have been wanting in the first place and you have released the worry energy – so you become light filled.

As you enter into this state again you will be met by a vibration of light, this is another aspect of your own soul, this is getting closer to Source but it is not the source of who you are for you could not manage that level of power so it has to be lowered down into a vibrational match with you as you are at that moment but remember in that luminous field that is around you that you have just transcended through, that is the memory field. The emotions that you have been emitting on the earth have not vanished for as we have stated before everything that has ever been put into existence will always be in existence so you meet the mind frequency of your own self at this point. Along with the mind you get the emotional energy of that feeling, now you have to marry the intellect, the knowing energy of the soul, with the emotional responses of the life, the two do not match, the two very rarely ever match for it has been an incomplete process.

As this awareness comes to you, that little point of light in the distance starts to meet you, it comes to you and it is now in front of you – how you will see that will be very dependent on how you view this through your mental field but there is one thing for certain – the idea that I did not achieve what I set out to achieve in this life will not let you go, it will wake up and it will start to permeate through that higher part of your mind field. The emotion will then come in and the soul quite often feels a great deal of sorrow, of emotion, of physical pain, it remembers, it sees, it reviews, it stands and it watches as it is a part of, there is no separation.

Think of it like almost being held in a magnetic field where you are being surrounded by a light spiral and you are spinning and spinning and you are experiencing all of what has been and all of what you have done but you are experiencing it from every angle, from everybody's experience, from the soul group experience. You are experiencing it from every direction, up, down, to the side, within and around and this causes the soul grief, not grief as you would see grief on your earth plane but grief in the knowledge that it caused harm to another soul, that it did not manage to meet the essence of the journey it came to take.

Now that soul with this new awareness and understanding of the cosmic blueprint and plan for the entire oversoul decides "I must return" but it cannot return for it has only just begun the journey into the hereafter as you would know it. Now the reality strikes the soul – "what is the quality of the life I have lived, did I live with a vibration of anger or hate, did I take and did I hurt or did I live with forgiveness and love in my life, did I have a weave of the two, was I loving to certain people, experiences and angry and hateful to others or did I live my life with a beginning essence of anger and confusion and work my way through into more peaceful love and light"?

As the soul actually goes through this experience of negotiating and understanding, it now becomes aware of where it must spend its time but there is no time, we will get back to the "no time" in a moment. So that we can better explain it we will have to compartmentalise it for you, you have now become conscious of what it was you were emitting, now you will go to where you vibrationally match and if it has been a selfish life, this match will be of a lower vibration, the lower vibration is a slower frequency. This slower frequency has more weight, it has anguish, it has the emotions that match what you have given out but this time you will experience being on the receiving end of what it was that you projected into the earth.

So now you find yourself in the recipient energy and you must stay in that recipient energy for you must fully understand the weight of burden of the experience that you have projected onto other people within that life but it is not punitive, it is not to hurt you but it is so that you get woven into the fabric, that vibration and that lesson that the soul needs. While it is in that state you have choices again as to how you will spend that time – most people when they go to the lower energy field of the earth and the afterlife are usually so disillusioned, so fully separate from the higher self that they cannot see it, that they do not separate it, that they do not understand it. When they make that fall from on high to the lower vibration they then get immersed in that consciousness, they will find their anger begets anger, they will find themselves consumed with that vibration, they will have to go through this, they will have to feel it, they may even try to access the physical world of consciousness in that state where they feel that they can again play a part in the life that they cannot incarnate into yet but again that is their choice, for if they choose to do that, we are now going to call them "the lost soul syndrome".

They are not lost for ever you understand but they are lost

into themselves, they have lost themselves to that vibration and to that energy but if you do not fall into that category, you will be sent to very much like your physical life circumstances, so you can experience and live life – this is why we call it the afterlife. You will find yourself meeting, working with and being surrounded with those who are a vibrational match to you who have been on the earth plane and as you experience those people, you are the recipient energy remember, so the recipient energy must receive what it has given out. As that person who comes to you, that soul, that spark, gives you that energy, you are returning that to them so there is a perfect harmonious balance achieved and as you work through each level, at some point that energy pull, that perfect union, again as you would on the earth, you pull yourself apart and you say "I will do this differently today and I will change this" and in that moment this is where you affect the change of the soul, not the life of the soul that you have come to know but the blueprint of the oversoul and the higher aspect of the self.

Now that higher aspect of the self can actually meet you on a slightly higher vibration because you are always nurturing your lower aspects of yourself – that will come in as a point of light, it will come in on a slightly lighter vibration and that energy will ascend to that slightly lighter vibration. As the other life partners and the other people on the earth of the oversoul have come back to Source and are going through this pattern within their own consciousness and within their own individual experience, that oversoul group that has met in that previous incarnation starts to ascend to this higher point of light. As the aspects ascend into that point, a higher frequency of the self meets it, it meets it with instruction, it has been given as the Lords of Karma, it has been given as the judicial system of power, this is how you may see it, because you are lower frequency you are still governed by that which you have experienced on the earth.

So you may set up a program of the oversoul to appear like, we would say if you would go into the ancient Greek and the Senate and the way that the judicial system worked there, you would have an oversoul group of souls sitting on the steps of consciousness, they are viewing down and looking at this soul, this individual aspect. It is looking at this individual aspect of the many parts that have been incarnated, although they are all interwoven, they are still individual and experiencing their own level of conscious awakening. As you start to draw closer together it is like ten points of the star all coming together, it is like that star conglomerate to make the whole, now that soul group is ready to pick up the incarnation process, it must put into place the brickwork, the framework of the incarnation. It must put into place the birthing of the parents, the siblings and the experiences, now some may not be ready to incarnate at that time for you are not meant to meet until you are of a certain age on the earth.

That person who you are meant to meet will have their own individual conscious light until these two points meet in that conscious union, now you have set down the seed for the incarnation process, now you have transcended through that darker side. You have the benefit of the wisdom of the life experience, the benefit of the wisdom of the afterlife experience and now you are in a vibrational match to come back to the earth but you may not go straight away for you may decide that you will stay for a while and you will help those who are on the earth plane connected through your soul. You may appear to them as helpers, you may appear to them as loved ones for there is no injustice, there is no judgement, there is no looking at any aspect of the self with indignation or anger or upset, it merely is what it is, it is completely impersonal and there is no outcome projected.

Even though you may look at this and say that this is a lower aspect of the self, it is still a higher aspect of the whole and it is still a higher aspect of what you will see happening in the earth plane until it again descends from on high into the earth. This Adam and Eve that you have been learning about through centuries is truly the whole metaphor for this for in this state you truly are in a state of complete contentedness because in that state of the afterlife you do not have judgement, you do not have your expectations, all you have is the instantaneous moment, that moment of creation, the all, the beginning, the middle and the end, there is no sense of time, you are timeless.

Although this is happening as you may say in the earth plane over a hundred years, it will be a mere light flick for you, it will be a mere reflection, and it will be a mere instantaneous moment. You will not separate the time on earth from the time after, you will not separate any part of that, it all becomes one for it is all happening at once, but there are many levels to time. There is relative time as you see it, it is that part of the physical that is orderly, that one foot before the other, mile upon mile upon mile, distance comes into play, time and distance and time and movement, this is what you are governed by on the earth.

You are not governed by that on the etheric level, you are not governed by that as you venture into your afterlife, you are instantaneous so you are not limited by a time consciousness, you are not limited by any aspect of distance and what you have to achieve, you are contented, you are happy to sit at where you are at that point but you are always working to progress your soul, it is not external progression, you are not looking for the approval of others, you are merely in instantaneous gratification for that process of unfoldment at that moment.

You look at time and you look at the earth and you believe that time has marched forward but in reality everything that has been happening in the afterlife is still an aspect of that part of the soul that is on the earth plane for you have never fully left the earth. No soul can leave the earth, once you have started the incarnation process you are always connected to the earth, what you are is a tapestry, you are a construct of reality, you are a conscious aspect of the Divinity, you are that field, you are that matrix.

We have always spoken of the matrix, there is no separate field, so the people who are living on the earth as you are at this time are as much a part of the afterlife as what you are in the earth, you just merely have the illusion of being separate, of having a different sphere, a different plane of reality. As to your question of *"are we all connected and for what purpose have we come into each other's presence at this point"*, as for that which you have spoken with the instrument, we would say to you that if you are in each other's presence, if you are in each other's part of the life that you have created, then you are exactly that part of the oversoul, there is no separation between one or the other, that you have lived lives before, you will live lives again, you meet after you have left this life and you will reflect on what it is you have done, you will see what it is that you are doing in this instant but there will not be a time or a distance attached to it.

> *(Carol, Mary and I had been discussing before the session about how our paths had crossed and that there must be a reason that we had done so and that perhaps we were all part of the same soul group. It has become obvious to us that those in the "Spirit world" are listening in not only to our conversations but also our thoughts.)*

When you meet you may meet the afterlife before the instrument, however when the instrument comes over to the afterlife you will all review what you are doing in this moment and there will be no time separation, it will be as this is happening in this moment for you will reflect and that will be that consciousness that is sparked in that meeting and in that union again. Does this help you to understand this question? *Yes, thank you.*

We understand that you cannot fully understand on any level what we are actually speaking of for you are limited by your time but time is relative. So now you have gone through that process, this is the average process for the average person as they lived the earth life, incarnation to incarnation. When you go into your past life regression, when you go into your past experiences, this is what you are doing, you are merely opening the memory – now is the memory still existing in this moment?

If you remember a time, if you land in another time zone of the earth, is that time still existing, is it still happening or are you merely reflecting back through linear time? Well there are two aspects for you may have one aspect that seems that you are not actually physically experiencing it and yet you will physically experience it in that moment through the mind field, through the mind, the intellect. It is still happening in that moment as it happened at that time on your earth but you have to move forward, you have to progress but if you were on the afterlife side and you chose to access that memory, you would be able to join and connect as you have done while you were on the earth plane. You could actually experience and go back to sit, to amalgamate, to imprint yourself into that experience and you could again live that life if you chose to and it would be happening in the consciousness as real as this life that you are now experiencing in this moment as you sit to work today – you can choose to do that.

The time that we are talking about does not run from back to front or side to side, it does not move forward, it is horizontal time, it is the time where there is no time, it is the time of all and All is One. Everything that is on the earth is happening at exactly the same time but you will visit another reality, you will visit the horizontal aspect of time if we could put it in that language. The horizontal time frame means that you can move through each layer of your own experience, each layer of the mental field and the layer that you will access as a physical experience is the connection where mind meets emotion.

The emotion that you placed on the earth while living that life is as accessible to you when you have left that life; but have you left that life? We think that you have not ever left that life for that life is still relevant today but we do not feel that you can fully grasp this concept and this is something in the New Age coming to you, you will become more and more conscious of because if you can move back into a life already experienced, then it makes perfect sense that your horizontal lift can lift you into an experience that you have not lived, and take you into a time frame which you believe is in front of you – but is it in front of you or is it actually existing in this instant but you are not a vibrational match so you cannot access that until you have left the physical body, until you have separated the outer shell but when you move through that time into the future and you imprint into that, is it that imprint and is it physical? Will it feel as heavy and weight-filled as this life, we say yes.

Can you understand what it is we are trying to articulate to you today? *Yes, thank you it has been very informative.*

Now we will talk about when you move into the afterlife and you have lived a life that you would say is pure evil for although there is the God force, there is also the evil side. The evil side is the heaviest, it is the one part that has the most density, and the evil side is the tumours, the growths and the illnesses in your body that is the point that manifests through the negative frequency. There are those who choose to spend eon after eon working to weave a darker mass, there are those who have made a conscious separation into the depth of the darker side. As there are many on the earth who are living to go to the light side, there are as many on the earth who choose to stay in the dark side. We have addressed the light side, the consciousness that wishes to progress forward, the aspect that we have described in the light side, the same dynamics play out in the dark side - time is still relative, however the vibration is slower so the illusion of being timeless is far, far slower.

When we talk about the dark side we do not talk about the hell process you are talking about, we are talking about control, manipulation, greed, hate, anger, desire and passion – will you recognise that in your own consciousness, will you acknowledge that for every part of you that is working to the Light, there is a counterpart of you that is working within the dark – which one is more relevant? Which one is more a part of your consciousness? You would like to see the light side of your nature, of your soul and when you see the dark manifesting in a fit of rage, it is so easy to overlook – this is what they call the devil, this is what they call illusion, seduction, this is the energy of the dark side, the force of darkness that makes mankind animalistic in nature, the very depth of its soul for if you did not have this aspect you would not have your light aspect.

The energy of temperance is like the river flowing in the middle, the wave of consciousness that separates the two but the two are never separate – which part of the river do you paddle down? Some choose to stay engrossed and contained in the dark side, they like to cause mischief, they like to conjure, to create hate, and they breathe hate into the souls of the dark side who are living on the earth. They whisper the negative thoughts, they whisper "kill that person for that person does not wish to exist" and the person who is tuned into the dark side of their nature will hear that voice more clearly than someone who is living with "I forgive you friend and know that you mean me no harm and I will merge with you and love you just the way you are and I do not need to control you, I can merely hold you with respect and admiration".

The dark side of the nature does not do that, it seeks to control, it seeks to hold and to manipulate, it seeks to guide for the self gratification. This dark energy pulls around, it makes you angry and you become immersed in the depths of your own despair, depression sets in, the "poor, poor me" and that can happen on our side as much as on yours. "It isn't fair" is often the language of the dark side, "why do these things happen to me" – this is the dark side that speaks to you. Most of us meet the dark side of our nature and transcend through those moments and hold the light for the light makes us feel uplifted but for those souls who bubble and toil and trouble and fester, they choose to stay in the depths and they do not wish to receive the upliftment, they are the dangerous ones, you have visualised them as goblins and ghouls and bumps in the night, they are merely the goblins of your own destiny and soul.

We ask you not to fear this energy for there are those even on the darkest of the dark who wish to become lighter at some point; these are the ones that we bring to you to help, to move forward.

They may not meet with us, they may not be able to stand our light, it does burn, so when we bring them through the physical being on the earth, your light is dim, that light can now manage to penetrate through that tapestry of weight, of darkness, of toil and of trouble and then they will begin the process that we have spoken of earlier in this session.

> *(Carol and Kevin, her sister Joy and her husband Steve, Geoff, and Mary and I meet in Carol's sanctuary on a regular basis to do "rescue work". That is we assist earthbound souls to go to the light and pass to the "afterlife". And from the previous paragraph it can be seen that we are not alone in our efforts.)*

True evil is a movement throughout the tapestry of the entire earth, there is not one race more evil but one race may pull to them the energy flow of the dark side to reflect the light of the other side, however we would urge you before putting labels onto communities and countries, for what is perceived as dark in one country and light in another will be the absolute opposite reflection to the people who are working within that connection. You have this happening on your earth, you have West, you have East and the two are reflecting, the West will see the East as dark, the East will see the West as dark, they are both aspects of the dark side and the light. This is this evil manifesting on a more global, on a more community base on that consciousness of the masses but this could not be reflected if it was not in the consciousness of the individual so the individual creates the mass, the mass creates the pull and the pull reflects the dark and the light. The dark and the light are merely a representation of the individual aspect of the consciousness of the people of the earth who inhabit at any one time.

Remember that we have said there is no time so as you move through and you vilify one and they vilify the other and as you work within that construct there are many possibilities that are being bred and manifested in that moment. So you will look to the individual home, the individual person, and the individual child to get a reflection of what is happening on the mass scale. If there is change to one soul who incarnated onto the earth and now becomes a vehicle of light to mature the darker aspect of the animal self and now vibrates on that frequency, it can change the entire outcome of the two nations which are a reflection of each other.

The more people who join in this light and release the darkness on both sides, you understand that it happens on both sides, this happens as a two-way street for the one who is on the West who wakes up and sees themselves in light and forgiveness has a counterpart to the East and the East will then match that and so forth. This is the tapestry that we speak of when we speak of creating peace, this is the power that you have within your own consciousness. This is a very important part of the message today, we want you to see this for I am the matriarch of the dark and the light, my orb, my light as I stand within the lake of eternity is that passport part, that essence of the transitional energy and as I stand you may see me as a wall of water between the two nations that are in your earth at this time - the two parts of the earth as I stand before and say to both, as I have no front, I have no back, I have no up, I have no down, I have merely a reflection on either side.

Will you not see this consciousness, children, will you not look through that lens, will you not change the view, will you not see each other as a reflection of love – if you can do this, you will change the outcome. At the moment we are in great turmoil for we do not see enough of the change, we do not see enough souls merging through the dark side on either side – we urge you to get this message to the masses, we urge you to help people to understand. If they wish to become more powerful beings on the earth and change and affect and consciously co-create, they will have to make the shift in their own consciousness and then the rest will follow – you make the choice but I am also a representative of the individual. As I stand between the masses,

I also stand between the individual from the light to the dark, I am eternal, I am all, I am soul and I have not come through to the earth before.

I have not come through because my time had not come but this time I must bring voice for I am not a soul as you would think of soul and few can manage my power, the power of the energy of the spirit that I work through has worked for long periods of time to maintain and withstand the frequency that I emit. This is the energy that I have to work with but between now and the time when the choices and the point of attraction come and there will be no choice left, my tears will be the river of destruction for you will pass your bullets through my water and through my water I will weep for your souls. I will take the earth and I will recreate it in the manner it should have been in the first place, you may destroy the earth at this time but you will never finish the process of the incarnation and growth of the individual soul, it will merely restart, re-manifest and we will work again in harmony and union.

Please understand that this is an impartial plea for unity for only in the unity of the whole will you find peace within your soul. We love you from our place in the Universe and we are sending our loved ones as this one is before you now to bring this message through, this is their job, they are the shepherds and there are many on the earth but their words have fallen on deaf ears. You will have famine, you will have floods, you will have quakes, you will have much turmoil because this is the turmoil which you contain within your soul and in one instant of your time on the earth you can change the whole.

If you understand what we have been bringing through today, the afterlife, the before life and the physical journey, they are all one and they are not separate. You are as much an aspect of the afterlife as you are the before life, as you are the physical life.

We will take our leave now if you have no further questions for us at this time and we will speak again if it is permitted.

6 - LILONG LI – AUGUST 29, 2008

*...I was known for my healing power but I did
not see with the eyes for I did incarnate into the
earth without physical vision, that was my biggest
blessing for I could not take the information that
would be through the visual senses and interpret
them in a normal way. The vision that I used was
the vision of the internal eye, it was the eye of the
soul, it was all expansive and although I never saw
form, I saw all living beings.*

It is indeed a real pleasure to be allowed to spend this precious time with you. At my time of passing I would have been known as ancient, I was the Temple Master, my name as I was known in this life was Lilong Li, this is how it was pronounced, I was a male in that life for it was only the male who could spend their time in such deep esoteric and spiritual studies. I lived in a very, very inaccessible mountain Temple, it was the Temple known as The Forgiving, it was the forgiving of one's soul for the express purpose of becoming one with the Source of all creation. I wore the robes of the anointed, the saffron orange and the beautiful brick red, the royal robes of the anointed, I was known for my healing power but I did not see with the eyes for I did

CAROL CRAWFORD

incarnate into the earth without physical vision, that was my biggest blessing for I could not take the information that would be through the visual senses and interpret them in a normal way. The vision that I used was the vision of the internal eye, it was the eye of the soul, it was all expansive and although I never saw form, I saw all living beings.

You will see the soul with the eyes and we will see the soul with the eternal eye of the All, the vibration, the colour, the pattern and when you see soul with this vision there are no limitations placed upon you. I could sit and read a book "The Thesaurus of the Oracles" was a book that I wrote, that I compiled and I did all without the visual eyes for as I have said, I saw with the eyes of the soul. This book was a direct link to the eternal, formless part of your being, it described how you were created, the spark of the energy that you were compiled, there are many levels of that compilation, they all work in straw mat formation with space between the layers and yet they are all unique and separate. When they are placed together they create a solid mass and this was the secret of the seeing with the soul.

We wish to talk to you about how you will get to know your soul – what voice does it speak and how do you connect with that part of who you are for this part is more real than all of the physical expressions throughout the eons. How do you recognise yourself as Source? How does this knowledge filter through and how do you bring this into the physical life? Over the weeks we have with many others discussed the intricacies of the very tapestry but now we wish to capture the sacredness of the journey.

You will know yourself as separate for in the separation of the physical life that you have now been born into; you will find yourself being drawn into the world that you are now a part of. This separation causes you much anxiety as you are a child – think of this anxiety as the very fabric of what you will experience throughout the threads of this life. If you were to look at a child standing with its mother and the mother or the security part left that child and went around an obstacle so that the child no longer

50

could visually see the security, that child would have a fright, a reaction to the separation and would let out an anxiety scream so profound that all of the security blankets within the vicinity would hear that pitch and respond in kind.

Think of your physical life as a thread on that vibration, think of all that you have experienced in your life from the time that you were a mere babe and think about the time that you first recognised that you were standing alone – feel the fear that sat within the very essence of your stomach. This is the anxiety that set the parameters for the entire expression and belief that you create within your life; this is the very essence of the tapestry. You have many fears and your fear of being alone is perhaps the most traumatic, the fear that you will not be loved but that you will have to face the world, this place of insecurity to you, alone and so you paint your first picture in the movement of your life.

With this picture being the first experience you then move forward, from this point you may not have such an extreme reaction but you will now set about creating the flow of your life at all costs avoiding that feeling and that experience, so you will bring to you all of the people who you feel will alleviate this fear, you will set up entire programs, entire families, entire friendships so that you will never have to stop and look at the picture painted in those first vulnerable moments. It is vulnerability that is the driving force throughout your life and your mastery of that vulnerable part of your being is the very reason that you choose to come to the earth and make no mistake that the very fact that you are in physical form is testimony to the power of your spirit and the manifesting nature of your being – you manifest and create all that you are experiencing.

When we were in the highest, inaccessible mountains we had no external stimuli, we had nowhere we needed to be, we had nothing that we needed to do, we had our religious studies (if you would put it in that context) and they were the studies of our very being, of the character of our soul, of what motivated us, of what fears we had, of the experiences of man, the beliefs created and we came through that painting and we had to address all of the areas that still were not in alignment with the outcome of the journey. We would sit in silence, this is a practice that you at this time do not find very enthralling, your entire structure is built on being distracted, on being busy, on keeping the pictures moving and not allowing the feeling to penetrate and address you and so you skip over and allow excuses for behaviour, for inaction, for all occurrences of your life you use the language of blame, you blame the external forces and you do not allow the very essence of your soul to speak to you. You know the power of your soul, you know the power that speaks through you and you know the potential that you will have to give away all of the earth distractions.

We are speaking about going in to the inner chambers, to the chemistry labs of your being, to the life that you are creating for you now have a truth that is graced in the earth that you are the creators of your lives but if you are creating your life and I am creating my life, how is it that we appear in the same frame, in the same experience, in the same time zone? You feel that when you leave the earth that you join spirit and you join those people who are already in the spirit realm but we say to you if you wish to understand the hereafter, you need look no further than the world that you are living herein for the world that you are living herein is a direct mirror of the world in the hereafter.

How can this be when there is physical form in one realm and essence and source in the other? Well, as much as you are creating your life and I am creating my life and yet we appear to be in the same moment and in the same picture of reality, the two essences, the two pictures have collided, they are matching and so we enter the other person's experience – it is the realm of experience that enters and combines and now we can form a relationship to one another. This is what we do when we come through a channel, we merely merge that part of the picture with the part of the picture on the earth and you will do the same when you move into the spirit realm, you will vibrationally match that place that you have inhabited while on the earth plane.

As we have discussed this in an earlier session we shall not repeat but we must say that from a spiritual, sacred place you are creating a temple of sorts, this temple does not have the walls and the structure that I was once a part of but it is a temple the same for with no vision the only temple that was accessible to me was the temple of my inner light. This was the temple that sought to encourage me to push through the boundaries of limitation and as I went through the limitations placed upon a physical entity and merged with the essence of my spirit, there was no separation and so therefore there was no limitation. As I moved through the order I ascended to the noble position and became the healer of the temple, the sage, the Wise Seer was the name that I was given for I could see limitless space and I could see all of your being, I saw this as you entered my picture and I became you. In that state of altered being I had accessible to me all of the memories, all of the experiences and all of the emotions of your life, this is what you are ultimately working to achieve as you go through each incarnational process, you are working to remove the physical beliefs and structures, walls that have been painted by the mass consciousness so therefore they must be real, laws imposed by the mass belief structure so therefore they must be obeyed.

At the start of each spiritual journey there is only one thing that is required for you and that is that you take all of that and you release it to the world and you come within your very being and you see with the eyes of the soul and as you do this all of the experiences, the chaos, the joy, all the sensory information starts to fade away. Now we come back to the child, when the child is born on the earth, it is born of pure innocence, there is no recognition of the individual, and there is no separation from the moment of reality that the babe is experiencing. This innocence is your spirit in its purest form, it is the gold and the grace of our God on high, this is when you are at your purest, formless, ultimate integrity, there is no negotiation between self and life, it is a combination of instantaneous experience. There is not another time in the birth process and life where you will be in this most pure form and present moment experience.

Now you are birthed into the world and you must meet that world for you are now a part of it and the first experience of being a self, of being an individual and being separate and having needs and being selfish, this is the birth of the ego and the personality. The personality has needs, has quirks, it needs for its own self gratification, it takes, it has a sense of separation from all who are around – I am no longer sitting in this moment, I am now separate from that moment. This is your materialism, this is your TV's, this is your clutter, your music, your driving from place to place and working for money and need and so the cycle of taking for the self begins – I need to feed my ego, I need money, I need the new car, I need, I need, I need, I want and I will have, I will divide and I will conquer for I am separate to my brother for he is different to me.

This is where your earth at this time sits from the birth of the innocent child to the selfish taking of the personality and the birth of the ego and materialism is born of the earth and distraction feeds your spirit. Now you must wade through the darkness of isolation and of fear for that fear of being alone, for that fear of not having your needs met, for that fear of death and separation is now the guiding light of your life and the driving force from eon to eon. As you transcend this selfish of states, you become one and you become master and at some point the journey changes and you are born into the realm of the third stage of your evolution, you become a giver.

When you reach that point of maturity, when you have gained all of the money, status and power and you are still unfulfilled, you will have to turn to nurturing your heart; your heart is the barometer of how well you have lived this life. As you turn to the heart, you start to uncover a far greater source of pleasure and you no longer wish to keep everything for yourself and the idea occurs to you that you may take what it is that you have acquired and you may share that with others who you perceive as less fortunate than yourself. As you turn from the need of the ego and the ego no longer runs your life and you hand over the power, you let go of the fear and you say "there is more to this than what I have been believing" and you become a creator in the most powerful form for as you create this belief you will be drawn to give back to the earth, back to your fellow man, now you have become a server, you are meeting humility, you are experiencing the joy of fruitfulness and you give this with pleasure and no ties of desire.

The third stage is the stage of the giver, the birth of servitude, your soul becomes what is important and you go within and turn away from the distractions of the ego and the sacred heart, the temple of your being awakens and you become one, a servant of mankind. The spiritual journey of the sage, of the seeker, the spiritual journey of man through the birth, death and resurrection and your heart, the heart is the temple, the all is put into experience and emotion.

As we sit in silence we go within and we hear for the first time the true voice, the intuition and now when those who are sent to you in illness and in weakness you are able to truly see them with transcendent eyes.

Have you any questions? *(See Questions and Answers)*

We thank you for your questions and we thank you for receiving us – May we give you the blessings of the eternal soul and may we wish you good tidings.

7 - FATHER BARTHOLOMEW – SEPTEMBER 11, 2008

...are you born into the body knowing that you will be a certain frame, have characteristics and a certain sense of genetic imprint"...

 Greetings – Father Bartholomew aligning up to the medium, to the vessel, bringing in the alignment of spirit with matter. It has been a very long time since I have felt the weight of a physical body and I must say that it does not feel very good, it is heavy and it is cumbersome and it feels quite limiting, so just allow me this time of adjustment.

(It took a little longer than usual for the entity to come through. Although this was the first time Father Bartholomew presented it was apparent he had knowledge of the previous sessions)

We wish to speak to you in regards to where we ended last time we met, you posed a question of biology, you posed a question of "are you born into the body knowing that you will be a certain frame, have characteristics and a certain sense of genetic imprint". I was far more scientific in my approach to human anatomy when I was on the earth plane, part of what I did was to map the actual anatomy, and I had a great fascination for the body and therefore have spent many, many lifetimes through many, many incarnations working within this field. I have studied the molecular structure, more recently which to your time frame would be – it has been studied in a more scientific nature but I will endeavour to speak to you on a more simple concept of your human anatomy, the genome, the biology and whether or not the genetic imprint that you are born with is actually the genetic code that you will experience in your life.

You are all working through the healing, the healing of your mind, body and spirit and we wish to take you into conception – you choose a parent and you say to that parent "I shall be born into your family, your family structure" and you impregnate into the mother's womb. Up to this point of your evolution on the earth, the only portion of this equation was that the mother was merely an incubator for that little seed that had been sown, you did not put very much importance onto the mother's emotional body and her state of mind, how she perceived the world that she was living in, the relationships that she had and all of this was very relevant as this incoming body that is incarnating into the mother is impressed by all of these, all of these external factors set off a chemical reaction within the circulatory system of the mother.

You will look at the placenta, you will look at that beautiful organ that is grown through the navel, and it is the one part of the body that every person and every animal that is ever placed upon the earth this is the connecting point to nutrition. This beautiful cord is very symbolic to us, it is representative of the silver cord that is connected like elastin as you inhabit the physical body, your spirit is on the outer part, it is still separate at this stage, however, that umbilical is not only connecting you to the mother if you are the seed in the womb but you also have the umbilical to the spirit, so the spirit is never far from the seed and the seed is connected to the mother. Everything that the mother perceives in her world will imprint through that connection, so we have a process where all of the nutrition, the nutrition that the physical body needs is transmitted through this umbilical cord and all of the waste is excreted through this cord – what does the mother do with waste? She takes this waste product and she filters it through her own biology, now as the mirror image to this, the baby, the seed, also takes in the nutrients and it is absorbed into the body and your modern medicine and your modern belief structure have been telling you that the mother only plays this role.

We would suggest that the mother plays a much, much greater role, the father is also a very important factor for if the father is upsetting the mother, then the mother is reacting to the father, then the father is reacting to the mother and the whole energy of the home environment that the mother is perceiving is in disharmony, dis-ease, that impression is then imprinted like photons of light into the very blood structure, it sends reactors, think of it as a reaction, through and into all the external glands in the body, the extreme reaction, the hypothalamus then kicks in and sends a message to the pineal gland. The pineal gland then looks at the world and says "is it safe or unsafe", if it's unsafe in the world outside it will send a message to the adrenal glands, the adrenal glands will then kick in and send hormones throughout the entire body to warn the body that there is a presence which is causing alarm – this will send waves through the blood. The hormones are carried into the baby, the baby receives the hormones and its own biology being that of the mother and the father, is highly attuned to this signal, so the baby will then start to react to the very essence of what the mother is sending in her alert system through the hormone release in her very blood.

The baby then lives in this state, it is supposed to be in a state of pure growth and the mother is supposed to be in a state of expansion, however, whenever there is an external that is not safe and the perception is that it is an unsafe world, this then shuts down the growth factor and it becomes protection. The alert system is then sent out and it states "shut down and protect at all costs" – the baby is then placed in this very mould – this is the environment which the child will grow in. All of the receptors are placed on high alert, now the body of the child will react to that and as a response, the back of the brain will then be stimulated, the back of the brain will stimulate a process of interpretation. If the interpretation is that the world is a safe place, that the mother and the father live in a harmonious world, then all of the blood signals and the hormones will be sent into this back part of the brain and the back part of the brain will focus on the intellect, the intelligence, the mind, the perceptive ability. If however the signal is telling the child within the mother that it is an unsafe world, then the blood and the hormones, the receptors and the chemicals will be placed into the front part of the brain, the front part of the brain is the behaviour part, so most of the nutrients in this state will then go into the external body, the external body shall be a larger body, that body is then programmed with the internal program of fighting, strength, determination, anger perhaps.

There is a whole process of a template that is placed within the behaviour program, so this child will possibly be the very child who will head off into the world with an angry, rebellious nature, the intellect will not be the central focus but the behaviour in the world will be that of determination and strength, that the world is an unsafe place and I must fight for my survival. The child who is brought into the harmonious home will be far slighter in build as most of the receptors have gone to the back of the brain feeding the intelligence, this will be the child who will be quieter, who will sit down. Now of course we realise that there are a whole load of other factors that come into play with this for there can be one bruiser in one family and in the other part of the family there can be a little mouse – how would we account for this? Well, the child and the situations that the mother experienced through each of the pregnancies are what is the individual factor, perhaps in one pregnancy, in one incubation period, there were times of life that seemed unsafe, however a few years have passed and the second child comes in and the mother is in a far more harmonious place within her own biology - you can see how you can get the two coming from the one family.

What does this really have to do with healing? What does this really have to do with the process that we came in to speak about today? Well, you look at your biology when we take it into the lab and you break it down into its very smallest atom to the cellular structure. You have a belief that your cellular structure is the construct of your DNA, of your double helix but we would suggest that this only has the program, this only has the stimulating factors in this process of creation so instead of looking at the DNA, we would look at the skin, the skin in the middle of the cell, that is the part that has the biggest role to play in the behaviour as to whether a child will come into the earth with a genetic default. We would say to you that even if you say that you have been born with a genetic default, that very often you have not and most of you come in with absolute perfection – there are the few but most of all are perfect in their creation.

So what happens when we say that we have a person who has a genetic default, well the program that has been getting laid down in the membrane, the receptors – think of it like this – think of it like a bread and butter sandwich, oil and water and polarisation of opposites you spread the butter onto the surface of the bread but they are still separate they have merely created a layered effect they remain separate this is the program blueprint that is being placed down and the cells are reproducing, all of the receptors are receiving the incoming signals – this is what is being placed down into the very cellular structure. If you want to create healing, this is where you must start, your receptors are much more contained in the cell as you would recognise them in your body, you have eyes, you have ears, you have senses, it is very much like the senses but it is on a molecular structure. When we make another sister copy of the original biology we are continually laying down those biological concerns, those experiences in utero, so a child learns through the experience of being incubated in a human body what the outside world will hold for them before they have even ventured in as the cells split and the body is created and the organs, all of this information is being received into the receptors and being laid down as the blueprint. That still does not give the whole picture – now we come into perception.

As the child is born, it is born into the world and it is born into a world of perceptions and beliefs, the parents' beliefs are the indicator of the child, now the child comes in complete, let us say our perception is that the child is born, the child is born in water, that a child born in water can swim, it comes to the surface, it breathes, it goes back down into the water, it has come from water, it has come from that very source, it is very comfortable in that liquid. Your cells are born in liquid, you are born from liquid, you come into a dry world, now over the course of a few years you have a response mechanism which matures but you have it from the moment that you are born, you can recognise your parents, you can recognise responses and you can pick up vibes – that's a bad thing to do, that may hurt you, the parent's face will change and the child will read the expression changes on the face of the parent.

As the child gets older and starts to toddle around you take it to water, it may be near a swimming pool, it may be near the beach, however all parents are on high alert – danger, danger, do not go there you could get hurt, you could die. The child reads the responses from the parents and then it takes those responses in and looks at the water and says "you could hurt me, I had better stay away from you". At just about this time the child then has a bathing suit put on it and is told "now learn to swim" and the child looks at the water, looks at the parents, then looks at the water and says "no, I could die, this is dangerous" so you have a perception sent from one generation to the next generation.

This is just one example of how perceptions and beliefs are transmitted from parents through generations but we would also say that this actually covers most of your belief structure, this is how we keep creating the world over and over, we live in the same world and yet we live in a different world, it is merely a perception, it is that ability to read the receptors and then bring that information in which is that process that we spoke about in utero. As you bring those responses in when you go through your life, you are constantly being exposed to new perceptions, new belief structures, you are being indoctrinated into a world that says "you must behave like this, you must believe this, there is this way of doing it" and you will behave in that manner. All of this is being impregnated in through those cells that we spoke about, it is being laid down in the very fabric, the receivers – think of it like antennas and as the antennas pick up the signal, those electro waves go into the cells and as they duplicate they then become the program. We are talking about the program, the program of health or the program of dis-ease, the program of growth or the program of restriction, protection, lock down and fear, both of these programs are working within you at every moment of your being – which one has the most voice, which one calls the shots?

As you are born into the earth and as your parents have been working with you to stimulate, to teach and to guide you, you are receiving all of these external signals. When you are but a small child that is what you are, one big tower of perception, it is not until you come into the next stage of your evolution where you start to become a bit more concerned with your own care that you actually stop being more reactive in the sense of receiving information and you start to express that information into the world. As the information comes in, the receptors are switched on so the genetics could have been that there would be an illness at a certain age or that there is a hereditary gene for cancer or you will be a haemophiliac, this may be very much part of the program that has been running through the parents' genetics and it may have been sown into the biology through the DNA and the cellular structure.

However, it does not mean that it will be replicated over the course of the infant's life and growth, this comes into the perception, what perceptions that child chooses to live by, this is more of the indicator, there is no real switching on but if your body is in a constant state of stress, a constant state of fear - now let us look at the external world, at your fear based culture – can you see the enemy or are they lurking in the background, do you feel safe in the world, will you have that job, the money that you need, will it be there, the home that you have, will you lose it, will the bad people come and take what is yours?   All of this is the body going in through that hypothalamus to the pineal through into the adrenals and shutting down the code, shutting down and holding in the nutrients - protection, sustaining, survival, fight, flight, movement, you cannot move forward if you are in suspended animation, if you are in fear then this fear, this stress is what is permeating and each of the cells, each of those antennas, each of those receptors are gathering in the stimuli that is coming from the body and the world as it perceives it.

As you would know this energy is far more highly charged, it is jagged in nature, the cellular structure cannot take that energy as it moves in this unaligned frequency, it just does not receive the signals, the signals are jammed, the responses for the amino acids, the proteins, the chemical workshop of the reproduction of your cells cannot take in this energy and so it is not reproduced in a way that is a copy. It is like a mutant and it mutates in its genetic structure and as it mutates it is far more highly charged and it grows and replicates, as this grows and replicates, it grows out of control – it is like a virus that runs throughout the body because the body is not growing forward, it is not moving, it is not moving into harmony and ease, it is moving through a program of stopping, protection, locking down, fear, anxiety, so therefore your cancer is born or your body reacts with pressure, the pressure builds and the volcano erupts and the aneurism, the blockages, the disharmony is now manifested into the world and you deal with the consequences.

However, if you are running a program of "the Universe is perfect and that there is no sense on any level that anybody can hurt you, that you are in alignment, that you have peace" then the energy waves that come to you and come in through your electromagnetic field and ripple out are far more fluid, they are a wave rather than jagged, that wave permeates and surrounds and the genes, the cells, the membrane, the receivers can take the information, the amino acids can re-duplicated, the sister cell in its perfect condition will be replicated in that mindset of growth and abandon abundance. We say to you that as you see your world, you are experiencing in every moment of your life this program, these beliefs and if you can understand that you perceive an idea and that idea only holds truth by the way that you receive that information, the filtration is then up to you.

Live in stress and live in fear and create disharmony and disease, live in abundance, live in that energy of expansion and growth, of excitement, of being happy and grateful and see the energy of ecstasy and joy fill your days. This is why there are epidemics of depression, this is why your schizophrenic society replicates the schizophrenic membrane and disharmony of the cells, the hypothalamus was never designed to be in a constant state of red alert through the nervous system. These glands were never meant to stay on all of the time, you are exhausting your neurological energy field, the channels and so you become exhausted and you cannot carry on and your life force ebbs away.

We will say that you feel that you are gods and you are able to now genetically modify, create changes in the food source, for when you pollute and mess with the genetic codes on any level you change the structure of the food chain. You cannot harness this power and the biology of the plant is based on the biology of the body, so from one plant on the winds of the breath of the mother, of the earth, is transferred like that imprint, like the perception to the plant in the next field which is blown and sown by the birds and the wind, it changes the very structure as your structure is changing - you were once healthy, you were once complete, you are now very much toxic versions of what used to be – majestic beings. So you are doing this to your plants and to your earth and hear this warning friends and hear it well – that the mother earth will not cease to exist for the genetic program of your earth is to survive, it will be you that the earth will eradicate.

There have been extinctions before, they have been from the stars, they have been atmospheric but we say to you, it will be your food for you feel you are God and that you can play God, you can take but we warn you the mass extinction will be through the famine of your world and it will be at your own hands. At any time you can change this for as you eat this genetic mutant food it also gestates in your biology, the micro-organisms that make up the balance of micro-organisms, bacteria - they mutate with it. So when we say that it will be at your own hands it will not only be from your crops but will be from your own bacterial sources for in truth you are bacteria - millions of micro-organisms conglomerated in one mass consciousness.

You are the earth - your New Age comes when you understand this.

Do you have any questions? *(See Questions and Answers)*

8 - LILONG LI -
SEPTEMBER 25, 2008

... Consciousness and unity – do you know what
conscious unity means and expresses?

 Greetings – we have met before a few sessions ago, you will remember me as Lilong Li and it is indeed a pleasure to again be allowed to visit with you. I am merely the first who wishes to communicate with you today; I am preparing the instrument so that when he who has been waiting to make this connection can finally meet with you. The instrument's vibration will already be accustomed to the higher, non-earthly vibrational frequency for the one who wishes to join you today is of a higher vibration again, he does not exist in the same plane where our consciousness of the Red Cloud exists, the cloud encompasses and moves through the sky and is made of all of the elements and I personally like this symbology and so like to work under the banner of that name.

Consciousness and unity – do you know what conscious unity means and expresses? It is the union of all consciousness; it is that point of the collective vibration of the earth, the collective output of all of the Divine individual sparks that unite in that macrocosm of the earth field and is filtered down through the vibrational light field. We wish we could show you how we view you when we see you from our side of life, like a pattern, a pattern of many bands where there is grey static patterns in between the solid bands, the light reflects the bands at its most concentrated point, you will get the speed and the colour frequency. Think of the rainbow and then think of between the two bands of colour, you have grey matter, that grey matter is fused with the colour from one spectrum of light and it unites to the next frequency of light. You see this as one picture but we see it as the two blending into one unity and this happens on the scale from zero to infinity, everything between the two points is working on a scale of perfection and union, slowing down and speeding up as it works in union with the other fields.

How do you make conscious connection to those on our side of life? You do this by using this analogy where you will lift up your matter and we will bring down our vibration and the two shall blend in a union and this is the point and the dance of creation, the connection between Heaven and Earth. This is what we wish to bring today as we speak with the Master, the Master has allocated a time today when he can join you. The instrument is constantly changing, the frequency between the bands of colour always rising and always drawing to one so the level of information that will be accessed is continually ascending and growing into the unified field of the cosmos. There is nothing that you cannot tap into for all knowledge is attainable to all but first you must be able to draw that frequency into your being.

When I spoke to you the last time we met, I explained that the life I lived at the time and the presence and feel that I bring to this meeting was working within the blind construct of no physical vision and yet at that time I told you that I was known as the seer and I could see your entire life, the lives you had lived, the life that you are experiencing and the collective field that you are emitting. There are not a lot of humans incarnate who have ascended to the point where this level of information is seeable, it is never seeable to the physical eyes, it will always be viewed through the spiritual eye and this is that point which awakens in the incarnational process to give you the second sight. You will all have an aspect which is awake within you but the maturation is the life experiences lived throughout the eons of your incarnations.

Each of you has had many incarnations. As we work we will not give any personal incarnational information for we do not wish to bring any physical associations with the ego and we are aware that the ego is engaged in past life recall and we wish to avoid associating any of you with grandeur. But we would like to share some information about one of the entities who works through the Red Cloud of which you will have heard and know of. The one incarnation we wish to share was known as the sage and was a Baal Shem Tov[2] through the mystical order of the Essene and was known before the times of Christ and has been handing down the sacred mystical priest/priestess knowledge. When we say priest/priestess knowledge, we will say that the union of the two vibrations in the one life was united so there was an androgynous energy that was created and we will say that this is when you will truly activate that kundalini, the energy and essence of the consciousness. You use the analogy of the serpent and we can use this analogy and it works fine but we feel it is of lightning and the pulse ascends from the base of the body and starts to pulsate through the energy channels, through the brain and the neurological impulses that govern your motor skills and movement.

When the kundalini is active, the two vibrations, the polarisation of the first and the second fields of reality is ignited and you have the gloom of the mass meeting the polarity of the magnetics. This is another step forward in the ascension to your New Age, you have not recognised that the energy of your kundalini sits dormant within the framework of the central channel of your being; you think that by meditating, that by touching and releasing the inner knowledge pull that you will access this level

2. Refer to the Historical section for details of *Baal Shem Tov*

of power? We say no for when you access this level of power you are accessing the God force, this force is life itself, it coils around your hips and it winds its way up through the memory reactor chips that contain all of the blueprints of your experiences and emotions and it is the emotion, that charge, the kundalini - this was the element and the essence of the book, the Oracles that I put to paper and wrote. As I gave this information to the world, the world remembered the sacred power and the God/Goddess energy and the Priest/Priestess initiation was ignited throughout the consciousness of the unified field and this message went out to all the sacred orders that have ever been created.

This is what is meant by the sacredness of your soul, this is the mystical side of your nature, you release and awaken the energy and you have called it energy and it is an electrical pulse, connect the electrical pulse from the base chakra and bring it up like a spring to the spinal cord, through the cord and into the brain stem. When the kundalini rises, this is the point of the axis of your being that activates the power of your spirit, through this part that energy is sent in pulsating, short, long - you created the Morse code, the beep, beep, this is a representation of that communication that is brought through these two points of your being, through the brain stem to the base of your spine, from the base of the spine to the brain stem, they work in unity.

As we said there is the rainbow of colours between and the place where the colours are most strong and bold and then the space between where the pulse rises from one and descends from the other to make the unified mass of the whole, the unified field of your aura. Where do you think the energy is amassed from? It has to come from some point, you emit it, and how do you think this field is emitted? It comes from above and is contained and moved up from below, there have been many, many who have spoken of these two forces, as above, so below, now we say as below, so above and as you emit this frequency, your feeling, how you feel in every moment of your being, that is what is being expressed – you know this as vibes.

You look at a person and you say "I do not like that person, they make me feel uncomfortable, I don't trust them" and in that instant this process has been pulsating that information of the emotion through this unified consciousness in the kundalini energy channel from the brain stem to the base of your spine. We have not included the third eye and the mental field for this is another layer that brings other information to the field, this is the point that you create - before you can feel you have to perceive, if you cannot perceive, you cannot have a feeling, from the feeling you give birth, from the perception you create the feeling and the feeling is your emoting. So the field is created by belief and we feel that we have already spoken a lot about the field of perceptions and beliefs, we wish to bring you the more spiritual, the more mystical side of who you are for you are this unified field and as you emote through this channel, you are emoting your spirit, you are emoting your sacred self, you are emoting the point of your experience through all of the lives that you have lived, through all of the lives that you will live and through all of the intelligence that you have drawn to you.

Now friends we have done our job and have ascended and lifted the frequency so that the Master will come to see and be with you today.

The Master Thoth – we have made the connection. Our beloveds, we are truly humbled to be in your presence this afternoon on your time. We have always been here but we do not take form for we are with you on all levels of your being but today as we meet with you, we will speak about your earth, we will speak about what you are doing to your earth and it is glorious for you are changing, you are growing. There have been many changes in the recent years so there is a lot of hope on our side that the changes that we see for your earth are now being activated, we say it to you like this – if you were to put the picture on the screen and the Angel of the ages was to come to you in this screen and take you by the hands into that screen, there will be a picture of consciousness projected from that image in your belief structure. As we take you through this picture, you know this as the dream state, the Angel of the ages comes to you and lifts you into the state of the dream world, you access the dream world, you move through the paradox of the physical world of the now present moment and move to the subjective picture of the belief program you have been emitting to this point in your development.

We take you into this picture that has been created – what do you think you will see? You will see destruction, you will see death and famine, you will see the limitation of the resources of the earth, you will see death for you know death as a physical reality, you will see pain and suffering, separation and loneliness for this is the reality that has been born, breathed, lived and experienced on the earth through man as he has evolved.

When you see this picture, it brings despair, sadness but we do not see this picture for from where we are if the Angel of the ages was to come and stand before you in the dream state, we could show you a new picture and this is the possibility of a shift in perspective of the unified field of the consciousness of the earth. We see a planet of plenty, we see joy, we see eternal life for we know no death, we see all of the needs being given to you in every moment of existence through experience for as vivid a picture of limitation is real for you, the picture of abundance and plenty is as much a reality and can be accessed at any point of the evolution of your species.

There are many who are on your earth who have a lot invested in playing the old picture and we say that the new paradigm is up to the individual to awaken the new picture and live in that experience, then the meek shall inherit the earth, the mammals shall be predominant over the fossil fuel of the past, it is in your own hands for as much as you see pollution, we give you perfection. You make the choice, you breathe the truth, you create the tapestry and the picture, you make the experience real, you will live it every moment with every breath - we give you unity.

When your body speaks to you, you do not listen so what chance does the spiritual side of your nature have to create influence in your being – if you have an ailment in your physical life, we say speak to that soul part of your being and release the belief and the need and experience the healing and the abundance of the love and joy brought to the experience of the union of the dis-ease with the harmony of your spirit – this is what the Master brought to your consciousness when laying hands on and making the dead rise. The belief that there was no separation and the words were with him when he spoke those words "it will be", it was done, it is complete, you are that God, I am that God, I am your humble servant and I await your instruction for what you believe and speak, so shall I incarnate into being.

When you understand this spiritual fact and live the experience as the Master of your being, you shall inherit the earth and the Kingdom of Heaven shall be restored to you, you were never separated from the love of the Divine Being of the Universe, you chose to forget your Divine majesty and being and experienced separation. This time of the picture being painted is simple, it is the remembering and the bringing into being of all of the elements of who you are in the remembering - we are you, you are us, no separation.

Lilong Li – we have returned. Do you have any questions before we finish our session for this day?

(See Questions and Answers)

We will take our leave now.

9 - SHISHILA – OCTOBER 9, 2008

*...that the New Age philosophy is actually one of
the most ancient philosophies that has ever been
placed upon the earth...*

 Greetings, it is indeed a pleasure to be with you
this afternoon as we find we are always very blessed
to be in your company each time that we meet.
We have met before and you have known me and
we have spoken at length, the last time I came in as
the consciousness forerunner when we spoke about the dark side,
when we spoke of the energy of the passing from one life into the
afterlife and the conditions of darkness that prevail at that level. I
wanted to come today particularly for I have a concept that I wish
to share and I am very grateful for being allowed this presence of
time to be able to share this.

My friend and partner who I worked with the last time that
you were together spoke about unity and consciousness and we
felt that this was something that we needed to speak about in
far greater context. This unity of consciousness you have now
come into and entered into the new state of awareness, we will
go through the language that this one who we work through
will use, this one has worked through the energy centres of the
Sanskrit and the very ancient esoteric text of the first seven energy

centres of the body. We have called them energy reactor chips, we will say that they are the closest to your physical body and live within the consciousness of that part of the anatomy. We have also ventured into the after death experience, the after death experience is where you will find all of the information pertaining to that energy centre that is not inside the body but is actually outside of the body.

You have come to understand that as counting from one to seven, you then move up to eight, this has been a language that you have now become very familiar with and are comfortable with, this is not a language that has been different from the past, it has now just been put into a context of understanding through your New Age philosophies but we wish to say to you that the New Age philosophy is actually one of the most ancient philosophies that has ever been placed upon the earth. If you truly wish to understand your Age of Aquarius as you have so aptly put it, please take a walk down through the winds of time, go into the time as you would have known pre-Christ for this New Age was birthed in that 2000 years preceding the Christ energy.

The Christ energy came in and he marked in a male consciousness, he marked an inward shift of perception, he took it from the Age of ram and created the age of the fish, the awareness of this age was, where the self fitted into the over all scheme your life. From the Piscean age we now say that you are moving into the Age of Aquarius. We like to look at it as the Age of peace for the Age of peace fits the very essence of the energy contract that you will be living as this New Age comes to greet you. When the Christ consciousness came into the earth he Heralded this shift, the New Age that he brought in was actually the finalisation of the proceeding 2000 years, and the birth of the next 2000 years, so you walk through an Age into an Age and you have a time frame of 600 years from the end of the previous 2000 years to the beginning of the next 2000 years, you have a 600 year window, three hundred years leading out of one millennium and three hundred years leading in to the next millennium at which time you have moved fully into that Age. As you live in this 300 time frame and move into the next 300 year time frame, you are in between the Ages, you walk between the Ages in this time – this was the time frame that Christ lived, these energies came in all around this time.

So you are now at that critical point, you are now moving from an Age into an Age – what does this Age have to do with unity consciousness – unity consciousness is the Age. Separation has been your recognition of individual self, you had to recognise yourself as separate, you see, in the Age preceding this one, when we say that you moved into a New Age, you actually were living the experience of a consciousness of connection through a physical door, however when you moved into the Age of the Christ energy, you moved into individuality so instead of the consciousness of the whole in a physical form, you moved into a consciousness of individuality and separation, you learnt to live a life of the self and the selfishness, selflessness, the self became the poignant part of the evolutionary scale. If you can understand this, then you can understand that there is global evolutionary shifts in consciousness but first you must be part of a tribal system, then you must move from that tribal system, you are now moving in that 300 years, you have been moving towards this time, you are in the second 300 years, you are coming in and have been in this space between the worlds.

What do we call this Age truly? Although we have said that it is more like peace, you cannot truly see it for it is not about you, it is not within you, we would say to you that if you really wished to understand it you are starting to create the technology of this energy in your world that you are living in. We would call it the Age of the Blue Ray, the Blue Ray you will now note is coming in on your machine level, it is always so. When you were living the Age before, you would have had the red laser, you are now in that space between the worlds with the Blue Ray energy, it is of a finer frequency, the Red Ray was of a more earthy frequency, the Blue

Ray is of a more esoteric frequency and peaceful nature. This Blue Ray, you may now understand it as we speak it because you have the machines that will interpret and work with that particular light frequency, however, the true Blue Ray will come at that time when the Ages are complete and the walking in the different Age spheres comes into a unity of consciousness and moves fully into that New Age that you have been talking about for many, many hundreds of years.

Now we would say to you that you will not understand this Blue Ray until it actually manifests in the sky, you will know and it will herald this time because you will see this blue star in your sky, the blue star is the point of the centre of the Universe and it has been hidden and obscured from your science and from your observatories by the Sun – it actually lives beyond your Sun. When this point beyond your Sun explodes or expands, it has been maturing, and it has been gaining in momentum for hundreds and thousands of years, your earth years.

The Cosmos is a time machine, you are one aspect of that time machine, you will see that star as a solar flare and it will be of the brightest of bright nature which will herald in that Blue Ray, when that Blue Ray filters through, it will be in a substance called radium, this radium will then encase your Sun, your Sun will super-heat, it will be as if it is caught in a blanket of vibration that is debris and heat, we will put it in that context. As it super-heats, it will then send out the solar flare, your planet will have this solar flare, you have been waiting and we have been speaking of the shift in your planetary system, the quaking of the earth, the movement of the species. This extinction will come in at a very quick rate but will take many, many decades to actually fully impact the earth, in our time it will be a twinkling of your eye. This will then send a cloud, a mass into the earth where the earth will be covered in a type of ash, you have seen it when we had our last big eruption and the whole earth was blackened, it is not unlike that. This chain of events are not set in stone, they are a vibrational match to the earth consciousness at this point in time. If you create a different expression of consciousness you will change the experience of the mass consciousness of man, and so you will experience a different outcome.

Now we would suggest that we have had miniature versions of this from within the earth and it is governed by the gravitational pull of the Universe, that mass of vibration that keeps everything in alignment, it is shifting, there are more and more galaxies being created and this is just one, like a needle in a haystack perhaps, there have been that many different galaxies that have been created. However, you are that one needle in that haystack within a cosmos that is so large that each particle of straw is like another part of the construct of the Universe, and so it builds out and out. Your little part of Heaven as you call it in this galaxy is mainly one little part of that, when you understand this, you will understand that it is neither here nor there in the overall scheme of the process of evolution whether or not you make it through this time in your history, for life will find a way and life will be recreated and there will be individual sparks that will be placed within the earth, we can assure you, so life will go on.

It will not take millions of years for this to happen; it will take a mere 100,000 years, in our time that is totally insignificant, in your time it feels like eternity. Now we come down to a unity of consciousness for there are elements of this that is the reality that you have created, this is the reality that you are on target to experience but what if we were to say to you that in the unified field of consciousness that in one instant, although you may still experience the Blue Ray, if you were to understand the significance and the changes that this would bring, then you would begin to prepare for that time in your planet history. So the magnification of what is to be done would change the perspective of the individual, the global consciousness would start to change.

We would say that there are four aspects to this understanding, you have the first aspect of understanding which is that there is only one consciousness on this earth, the second part of this is that there are individual aspects of that one consciousness, unity of consciousness, one consciousness in creation, and you are the individual aspect of that consciousness. The individual aspect of that consciousness breathes that part of their nature into the earth by prayer, it is quite simple, it is the spoken word, it is the mind thought, this Blue Ray is actually that thought process, it is in that prayer that you can do the changing, the changing of the outcome of the situations in your life whether that would be in a planetary sense or an individual experience – that is the third part of unity of consciousness. The fourth part of this great scheme is that when you move from prayer, you move into a space of completion, you understand that if you can conceive of it, it is already done and this is that part of the prayer that you have not had access to.

When we said where we started that you came in on the New Age and yet it was a very ancient age which took you pre-Christ, you will understand that back in those days that understanding of the unity of consciousness was how you lived your reality. In order to lose it, you had to make conscious choices not to put any more energy into that conscious belief so that understanding of your reality slipped into the winds of time, it has not left reality, it has just failed to remember and be active within that framework of your life.

This is the ninth centre – we shall place it into words that you can understand – the understanding of the afterlife condition, this is what is meant by the Lady of the Lake, the lake is the unified field and the energy of the lady is the unity polarisation of the male Christ consciousness that was birthed in that time for you had to walk a patriarchal energy experience and at the birth of the Blue Ray you will walk the feminine, so the person who will be born into your earth will have to be born into the female body.

We will explain unity of consciousness now from another perspective and it is in regards to the sacred feminine role of the next stage of the evolution of your planet for we will take a bold step and we will say that the male energy is actually slowly, evolutionary over eons of time breathing itself into extinction, its genetics are responsible in the chromosome of the Y and the X. The mitochondrial[3] DNA of the mother through the womb and through the genetics that are laid down – that does not change and so you can take the mitochondrial DNA and you may go through generation from generation to generations past and as long as there has been a female child born of that lineage, you will be able I assure you to take it back to the original mother source. The male, on the other hand, totally mutates generation to generation, there are certain seeds that are placed into the mix but the varying from father to son is of such a degree that the actual generation cannot be traced back. Now we have established the female – you begin your experience as a female and at a certain point of the evolution the chromosome changes and you get what you class as the male anatomy – that would be so.

Now we will take you into a dream and we like to use the word dream, we will take you into a situation in the Amazonian forests where there have been no males allowed to live, the males have been removed from the entire tribe and all that is left is the female. The females have been living successfully and this has happened on your earth, have no doubt, the male energy that is contained within the female ovum, within the egg, remember we said that the male only changes when it is touched by a certain chemical response and then your testicles will drop and the ovaries will remain and the male will be born and the female will be born into that gender. The males have breathed and birthed themselves out of existence in this tribe so how do the females continue to flourish? Do they run out into the world to collect males as their slaves? I do not believe this is so, what they learned to do as a group energy, as a unified field of consciousness is that they have

---

3. **Mitochondrial** – minute granules in living cells responsible for respiration and energy production.

learned the art of being able to touch the egg within the ovary to such an extent that the egg can fertilise without the need for the male ovum, at some point within the females.

So at some point when the males have begun to recede in the earth and I will say to you that there are more females being born on your earth today than at any other time, that you will find that in the eons of time and this you will not prove today and we cannot offer anything that will give you validation for this except to say that this is a part of evolution that will be brought forward onto your earth. The females will be able to do this and this will be a consciousness of unity that is born onto the earth but we have taken you into a dream for this is not a reality until it has been birthed into creation so we would say at that point that you would go into the book of dreams to the seven levels and that may be one of the chapters that is contained within that book.

We will talk about our friend who wrote that book of the Oracles and in that book of Oracles of creation, that book contained the seven different creations that are available to you within the dream world. This is one chapter of that book, this is not that far fetched for it has already been done in your laboratory, it has already been done by science where the egg has actually been touched in such a way that it has been genetically, let us say "fooled" into splitting and creating and when you understand that each cell, the egg is virtually a copy, for genetic blueprint is already there and you are designed to divide and multiply and cells grow into organs, you will see that this is not that far fetched. We would also say to you that as you walk into these dreams of possibilities of reality that you will be very challenged in your time for the Blue Ray of the New Age that will come to you will offer many possibilities and those possibilities will be decided by the unified belief structure of the mass consciousness within your earth.

So if you took it through the door of healing, as you go through the process of working with the biological body, you can understand that if you could change the process from being injured into being fully well, then you would begin the process of a consciousness field that would determine health but what would happen to the structures in your society that depend on misalignment and no health? They would then have to break down but if we said to you that this is already happening on your earth, these structures are what we call the dinosaurs, mass weight with no consciousness, they are only conscious of the self, they only feed the self in the instant moment. What if we were to say that another unified consciousness thought pattern would be that instead of serving the self for this moment in time, perhaps the more caring aspect of the mammalian nature would be the awareness of the entire process of the whole before the self, this is what the master Christ came to teach you. He is incarnating again, I assure you and I believe he has been in incarnation for a number of years but you have not recognised him within your philosophy for he is not to come in that context at this time yet, he is not to be the light to show you that field that he did in the past, he will not come in the same light, he will only come in under the banner of a light of energy and knowledge, it is the knowledge he will herald the New Age by speaking this knowledge, this is what he did in the past when he joined you and you crucified him. You will not do this in this life for this master will never again be made the martyr of an entire consciousness, instead this time when the master appears to you, you will know that master by the content of what is being given and by the abilities that have been shown to be used by that master. The master will be able to look into your agreement, look into your soul and be able to work with you on that level, that will be one level, there will also be a teaching level, there will also be a healing level, each one will incarnate at the correct time and this one is now working with that vibration so you can understand that the new Christ energy being birthed into the earth is that of the ninth centre that you would understand.

The ninth centre, unity of consciousness, remember there is only one consciousness within the earth so if that master is born into the earth then it stands to reason that the master is only an aspect of that consciousness of yourself and so will manifest in a form that will fit that time, it cannot be other, they will herald in a message that will be heard and it will be in the time when it is meant to be heard. So whether it is in this time and this space or not is not the important part for you may not recognise this master until long after the time of their own physical passing when they leave the earth for they will never be put up on top of the hill again so that they can be pulled down, that has been done. However, when you move into the afterlife, which is ridiculous to us, then you move into that full radiant expression of yourself, this is where I work.

There will always be the light of the light and the dark of the dark and if you want to cut through all of the words and get down to essence and source from the light of the Creator to the darkness of the dark, there are simply two words, the prayer and God force and ego and self, selfless and selfish, the me, me, me and the no recognition of me at all - you will understand unified consciousness, I will be sure to explain this. Unified consciousness is the perfection of the understanding of that which we have been saying that there is one consciousness that is created and the second part is that you are an individual aspect of that consciousness. The me, me, me has no understanding of that unity of consciousness and then we would take it from the dark of the dark to the light of the light and ask the question – where are you within that spectrum? Are you living the life congruent with the ninth centre awareness or are you living the awareness of separation and self, where are you on that line?

The third part is prayer – how do you respond to the people in your life for they are that unified consciousness, we would come into comfort, greed and profit along that line – will you profit from another's misfortune, will you walk over a person in order to fulfil the self, will you find compassion or will greed come into the equation? When you look at the other end of this line and you walk into a field of gold, this is where you would find compassion, this is where you would find unity, love, the idea of the sharing of the whole, this is where you would look at the person and say "friend, you need this, then it would be my honour to give you this, you need help, let me prop you up".

What is it that you need to bring yourself into alignment for in that alignment you will bring yourself into that alignment, it is all about the unified field, you have chosen the upper path and the upper path is comfort, greed and profit and as that line merges up it reaches stormy weather and eventually it will have to falter. The bottom of the line will reach the golden corn, it will be the field of plenty but where on these lines do they cross? – this is that 600 year point, where do they cross, where can you visit the comfort, greed, profit, where can you merge back into compassion, love and mercy? – the two over the eons of that time frame you will slip in and out of the ages of that overlapping energy. As that energy overlaps, eventually the lines become very distinct and the point of reference is when the two no longer blend but take a sharp change of direction, if this sharp change of direction comes about, then that is when the unified field, the head part, the mind part will separate from the body and the body shall perish, this is where you would see that cataclysmic reality taking place within your world, it is not to hurt you, it is merely that you chose the path of comfort, greed and profit.

If you then slip into the reality of compassion and mercy, then you will follow that line into old age, when we say old age, it is metaphor for maturity, the soul matures into the Golden Age, this would be what you would class and those yugas you were talking about earlier, the Bronze Age, the Golden Age, the Silver Age, the Iron Age. The Iron Age is the Age of destruction, it has the Saturn energy of fire and heat, as you move into the Blue Ray, you will move into another cycle of 2600 years, 2000 and the 300 leading out of that Age to the 2000 and the 300 moving into the New Age, the point where we started. Now you will have this happening on your earth and you will not understand it consciously, it is something that you do unconsciously every moment of your life, the two lines blend for one day you may be in a very generous mood, for another day you may be perceived as angry and moody, these are the differences of those lines and your unified field of consciousness within the earth has chosen the upper line, that upper line of comfort, greed and profit, it has not made the shift and the time of your Mayan calendars is that point where the two separate and there is a point of no return. When the point of no return comes, you will not see it as mass destruction on the day after, we have already said that, between the 12th and the 21st will be the window, that will be the time, we have had a 20 year cycle, we will then go into another 20 year cycle where we will not manage to make that overlapping shift into that time.

I hope that this has clarified what we have been trying to put together for you which is a conscious understanding of the new teaching for when you truly get this teaching, it has the potential to completely change the entire cement, brick fabric structure of your entire world. Just with one shift of consciousness you will move into - we will put it in the Book of the Oracles, the Book of the Oracles that we feel that you are writing now and the seven chapters within those different Oracle stages of evolution you are becoming aware of, you have done the choices already up to this point - now as you go into that dream state, you will then go in and you will choose from one of these seven chapters what it is that you will experience, your prophets of old did this, they did nothing other than this, they went into a different chapter, they saw a different outcome, the outcome that the world at that time had created in that unified field – can you now start to see that you have always lived this unified consciousness yet you have not recognised it.

The master who is here now to teach you is to teach you this awareness, in this awareness as that information filters into the more primal bases of your nature when it saturates you, it has the potential to change your entire world, the dinosaurs will die, the fossils will no longer take from the earth but the mammalian, the mammals, the caring, the nurturing, the female aspect will be truly birthed into the earth. Can you not see that the master of this age is the female, we are coming full circle into the age of the female energy, intuitive energy, intuition and sight and do not think that the patriarchal energy you have been living will not be implemented on every level of this new Blue Ray Age. The energy of the patriarchal was a mystery and a mystery school of thought, of life, of consciousness, it was the left eye, it was the eye of the male energy and it has been superb, it has been perfection, it has been exactly what it was meant to be, we celebrate the male energy.

When that male energy shifts from the red laser to the Blue Ray of the female intuition, there will have to be a time where the two fields meet, you have the Goddess worship energy of the time preceding the male where you would have called it paganism, it is that ritualistic female, my time of being on the earth, the Goddess, the Lady of the Lake, this is what I am, this is who I was, this is the reality that lived beyond the veil of the earth, I lived in the dream state, I lived in the power of the spells and the rituals and the women who made you healthy, I lived in that breath of consciousness. Now the patriarchal comes in and it takes you into a more reasonable, more logical time, it takes you into the depth of separation, power, control, it take you into that vibratory pond of energy and now the two powers that have lived throughout the earth merge as the Blue Ray of the New Age, of the unified field of male and female so the female eye of intuition is now opened and the two powers reside within the person, in both aspects of the individual of the consciousness – can you see how the potential for change keeps growing, can you see that if you take logic and reason and intuition and wisdom, Divine wisdom, sacred knowledge, ritual and you take power and control and you use that perfect harmonious blend of vibratory action and creation, you can truly create the Garden of Eden – this is the metaphor within your earth, this is the metaphor of the birth of Eve from Adam and Adam from the earth that he was created to live in, this is Adam and Eve, the Garden of Eden is here, it is now, it is in every cell, it is that two line system that is now going into a separate mode.

We believe from our side that these words being brought through from all of the different masters who were on your earth, we will say that this information is in many places on your earth, the more we can get this message to blanket and saturate, the more power it has in your consciousness, now we make the shift and instead of that energy taking a sharp turn with the line going upward, we walk through and we merge the two ages of male and female and we come into a unity of consciousness and empowerment that will truly take your earth into a space that it has never recognised before, it is already created within the earth, this is already a possibility, it is already a vision. There is one who has seen the vision, this is the prophet who will go into that time, into that chapter of that age, this is the new yuga that is being created, it is a powerful age and it will be heralded by the Blue Ray of the star in Heaven that will be that point of explosion that will change the magnetical shift of your reality in your earth and in your own polarity. When that changes, what you will experience will be what you have created – have you created the maturation and the golden or have you walked into and continued with the age of thunderclouds and profit and greed and serving the self alone or have you manifested an age where you will go to the light of the Creator and work with the unity of all beings for you will truly understand that when you kill one another, you may as well stick a gun to your own head for that is the price that you pay and it is a price that we would suggest is far more than what you could ever wish to inflict on another soul for that soul is you in a separate form on the earth.

Remember the master Moses who came to the earth and when he asked that bush "who should I say is calling upon me to be this prophet and to rescue and take my person, my people, myself from that place of enslavement", I responded "I am that, I am, I am you, there are no separations" and he believed that much that in that instant he created the "me" and "I" was expressed in the earth and then he had the power from within to move an entire enslaved people out of that place of restriction and take them to where they needed to be. It is a metaphoric journey that each Age, each place in your history will continue to repeat until the unity of all beings is created - this is the message from us for you today our dearest and beloved friends.

We wish to take our leave but we wish to advise you that if we are to continue with this we would ask that you understand that you are actually heralding in the new consciousness of unity and you will be the forerunners for the future but you are not new in this for this is an old, old teaching and it is the wisdom of the ages but fully expect to find this in many places – we thank you for your time.

10 - BAAL SHEM TOV – OCTOBER 23, 2008

...You have been living the experience of the physical of the male energy, you have been living the existence of the patriarchal system, the system that you have been living is the system of external power, the left Eye of Horus was the reasonable, logical and linear...

Greetings friends, we have been waiting for this opportunity this evening to come and speak and share this evening with you.

You have touched upon many subjects but the one that we wish to speak to you about today – first of all, may I introduce myself to you please, my name is Baal Shem Tov and I have not come through the medium up front and so I have stayed behind in the background, she has felt me but she has not actually brought me through on this level. I was a teacher, a teacher of a mystical tradition, that mystical tradition was birthed onto the earth but I was not a particularly intelligent man, I was more a being of light that was sent in to bring about a new level of understanding upon the earth.

Now this level of understanding has been brought through many incarnations since, it has been put down in writing and it has taken on a different level of understanding as I would have taught it, as I would have brought it through. I was not particularly interesting in my own life as a physical being but I was able to do what this medium is doing at this moment and I was able to channel an energetic pattern of a higher vibration and for this they called me a Master. However, I will be very, very frank with you when I say that the Master is merely the reflection of the student, the student will literally create the Master by the needs of that particular person who is coming to seek wisdom.

We were about to discuss with you when we decided it was time to remove the individual consciousness of the medium and we are talking to you about the ancient mystery schools which is quite relevant because, trust me when I say to you, that I did give birth to a level of this on the earth plane. This was brought through the Jewish philosophy, this was brought through and was actually harnessed into more of a dogma than a belief that I had adhered to while I was on the earth but that is not what we are actually talking about this evening.

What we are actually talking about this evening is that we are going to go into the mystery school of Horus, the birth of the god from the Isis goddess, this god that was born, it is not necessarily a human god, it is an energetic god, you will call it god but it is not god. So we brought this through on a level where we have two eyes, now this we need to bring back into the consciousness of the masses for you have not understood that you have only been living one experience of this mystery school. You have been living the experience of the physical of the male energy, you have been living the existence of the patriarchal system, the system that you have been living is the system of external power, the left Eye of Horus was the reasonable, logical and linear. You had to walk through this door for walking through this door allowed you to walk through a time on your earth where you would put all of your own power into the world in front of your eyes, ultimately this power was created so that you would give it to others, it was the power of others over the power of self.

This may not make total sense to you but I believe as I walk through the world of your experience today that this understanding is being birthed on a new level. There seems to have come a time when the earth people, humanity, the human kind, they are now beginning to understand that it is not about looking after other people, it is about looking after and being selfless. Now this may seem as a paradox for we were just saying that as we birthed and became aware of external power, we gave our power over to the external masses, we gave our power over to the outside world.

In order to give ourselves away to the outside world, we had to go through a door that said that we were not necessarily good enough, that we did not measure up, that we were not able to perceive ourselves as Divine beings but we were merely these aspects of an imperfect being. If you would look at this, you would see that this is not possible for the only things in creation are in perfect union, there is nothing that is ever created that is not in total harmony and perfection, it is merely the belief of the person they bring into being with their own belief structure. So this was this ancient wisdom, this ancient, esoteric knowledge that gave birth to the left eye of logic and reason and the patriarchal power system.

Power had to be taken from the person, the individual and be given to the masses, the Government, all of the powers that be let us say. However, the time on your earth is shifting very quickly; we call this the sands of time, now the sands of time simply reflect what you are, look at a single grain of sand on the beach, it can be picked up individually and yet when it is placed back onto that surface, it is lost in the masses of the other granules that become the mass, that is the mass that is separated as your feet touch the sand. You do not differentiate the individual grain, you do not feel the individual grain and yet when your foot is placed on the sand, the surface of the sand you feel as solid, this is the new power that is being born into your earth, it is the understanding and the recognition of the consciousness of the masses, it is that one unified field.

Now you have had many who have come onto the earth who have wished to discuss this but there has been a limited understanding, so now we will say that we will give birth to the oldest and the rarest at this time on your earth and this is the right eye, this is the right eye of Horus, the ancient mystery school that has been forgotten through the sands of time. This school is teaching you that you may be an individual aspect but there is nothing individual about you, this is what we were talking about earlier when we were talking about time, it was said that there was no time, that there was no time in the past, there was no time in the present, there was no time in the future, time is actually like a stream, it is constantly moving yet it is never moving in a way that separates it from the whole, it is always moving in a unified force.

The individual water droplet becomes the river, becomes the ocean and then that becomes the earth as it is brought from the sea and it is placed into the air and it is created through the clouds through the evaporative process. So you get to see the birth, the death and the recycling of your own individual consciousness, your own individual spark, there is nothing on this earth that has not existed before that will not exist again, nothing can ever be lost, it is only in fluid motion and in transit. You are that divinity and when you understand that you are as powerful as anything that has ever been placed upon the earth, you will start to see yourself through a very different lens.

When we say that there is a new mystery school that is being awoken within the earth, we would like to break it down individually so that you may get a sense of how you can become more empowered in your every day life. We have talked about the lines in previous times when we have spoken through the medium but this is the way that we would discuss it today – you have the light of the Creator within each of you and you have the dark of the Creator in each of you, you have both elements of that Divine Source as it runs through your being. You are creating the reality of your life every day that you are in existence but is it the existence when you are on the earth plane or is it the existence when you are in the infinite realm?

We would say to you that you are creating the physical reality while you are still in the infinite realm, when the medium says that you are mostly out of form for most of your life, that you only have that very small aspect being birthed into the earth, you will get a sense that you are totally spirit, you are totally vibration, you are light, light runs the Universe, light creates the Universe. You have the belief that there is a past, you have the belief that you are sitting in this moment and you have the belief that there is a future awaiting you tomorrow and what we would like to bring to you is the fact that where you are sitting today is a reflection of what you have lived and believed and experienced in the past.

There are many layers to this, you have seven layers contained within seven layers, we call this vertical time, from where you are standing at this moment you are the sum total of all of the experiences that you have lived and the vertical time is that space where you are sitting in the present. What you are actually vibrating and creating is a reflection of what you believe in this moment – if you believe that you can connect with a higher vibration, if you believe that you can be an instrument for the Divine Source to flow through, if you seek the teacher to teach you how to align to this belief, if you create the experience and if you go through the process then the future will be that on some level you will be working to connect with loved ones who have left the earth. Now, how you do this will reflect how much of yourself you will put in to this process – will you do this because it is an interest that is a passing, fleeting moment so that it is a new toy that you can invest six months, a year and then you go off and you feel it is complete?

Will you create the next level where you may spend many years learning to fine tune the skill and working with those who are being sent to you and being committed and dedicated to the process for if you stay in that vibration then you will attract on the vertical time frame a future which will allow for that possibility?

You must be aware that there is nothing that you cannot create, it is simply that you do not wish to put that much of yourself into the process and yet from the lowest of the low to the highest of the high potential you have accessed that in any given moment of your created life.

We would go into the belief that when you wake in the morning and you place your feet upon the floor, the floor beneath you truly is a solid entity because you believe that, when you walk into the mirror and look at your reflection, you truly believe that you see yourself in that mirror because that is what you have been taught and that is what you believe – you are consciously a vibrational match to that possibility. However, if you have been brought up with the belief that there was no such thing as a reflective surface, then you would not be able to see the image of the self in that substance because you have not recognised the pattern, it is not something that you can actually visually tap into and actually create a belief structure.

When we bring that into your health, you can start to see that this has a very, very rich application, so when we are creating a religion, when we are creating a system of power, that system of power is merely the reflection of what it is that we have chosen to recognise as the individual pattern and if we could not recognise that particular pattern, then we would not create that experience. If you wish to choose a different path, it is not a case of choosing that path out of feelings that you have done something wrong, it is more a part of recognising that you have done everything right to this point in time and at this point in time you have now outgrown that belief structure and the beliefs that are now coming to you are the beliefs that vibrationally match where you are in your maturation today.

You have a vibration that you have not been introduced to – you are aware of your auric field and you have discussed this tonight so we will not tap into that source at this time but what we wish to bring to you is the Torus energy and this is the energy of the creation that you are now birthing into your earth. So this new consciousness that is being awoken within you resonates from within the heart, you have been aware of the physical form that you have manifested into life and you have been aware that there are four levels to that which encompass a lot of vibration and a lot of light and energy working in unity to create that unified field of experience that you call your body.

The energy that you have now become aware of, the Torus field is like a donut, it has a hole in the middle and it circulates, it goes around and around, think of a spring, think how it is a continuous coil of energy, this is what the time between time consists of and from your heart place, that beating, pulsating, magnetic connector to that vibration of possibilities – vertical time, you create your own reality. Now there has been much talk of this in your earth plane and yet no understanding of how the concept can actually be created in your own experience, so we have decided that it is time that this energy field is now brought to the masses for the unified field of consciousness has to change in order to affect the changes that you will need as you move into this higher vibration in your earth.

So be aware of this Torus energy for if you have an idea that I would like to be a medium, I would like to be a connector to those who have gone before, for those who are no longer in form and for those who remain on the earth at this time, then the energy of "how well do I wish to achieve that which I have put the intention to, do I want to be mediocre, do I want to visit it when it suits and then get back into the distraction of the life or do I wish to put an arrow of intention into creating a vibration link that will make me be the highest of the high in this realm so that I may make the finest and most subtle connection to those who come and to those who have been left behind – how do I wish to do this?

Through the Torus energy you will create that experience so if you wish to be the highest vessel and you hit the higher altitude of that vibration that you are magnetically attracting to yourself, you have to put the intention, you have to put your belief into that process, you have to then take action, the action is then what creates the magnetic connection to bring that to you. We would say that it is the same with money, with health, with relationships, you can apply this to every area of your being. We know that this is of great interest to you at this time because there is a lot of murmuring within the collective field of the earth, you do the affirmation, you do the work that you feel will bring that to you and yet, like a blackboard, after you have written it ten times, you then spend a hundred times wiping it out and then you wonder why that tutorous energy cannot bring that to your field.

Please be aware that this is the essence of the mystery schools of old, this is the essence that was lost when the patriarchal system of external power was born into the earth for you had to give up the power of the self, the individual self, that self that is divine in nature and you had to put yourself into servitude to external power so you became very much a vessel, a vessel of disempowerment to your own life and to your own self, you became sheep that followed the shepherd. We tried to send in many over the course of the eons of the time on the earth to help you to remember who you were, unfortunately the track record for the earth is that if you do not understand then you had better shut it up because if you do not shut it up then it can absolutely create ripples, havoc and chaos.

My goodness, imagine if the individual woke up and saw themselves as divinely powerful as the Creator of their own being but better still if they had a working understanding of how powerful they are and just how they go about creating this force within their own life, then the powers of the external world, the powers and the Government, the leaders and the dictators would instantly lose all power over you and this is in essence the New Age being born into your earth – this is what it is all about.

We sit here with a smile on our faces, if we had a face, because we would say to you that in creating the New Age you are actually awakening the oldest and the richest text knowledge and esoteric mystery schools of eternity, this knowledge has been inherent since time began on the earth so in the New Age you are accessing the old system of power that has always been open to you, you just could not see it because you did not believe it and you could not magnetically, connect it into your consciousness.

Would you have any questions on this or any other subject? We will take our leave now and we thank you, God bless.

The winds of time has been spoken of much tonight, time is of no consequence to those in the spirit realm, time shifts, time stands still – I started thinking about the physical and that has brought me back, I could feel a tugging, I felt that there was so much to say.

Carol Crawford

11 - PAUL – November 6, 2008

*...and why would you bother to even start the
journey from pure Divine Essence, perfection you
might say, into this less than perfect instrument
that inhabits the earth?...*

 Welcome to you, it has been a while since we have
sat together in this place. There are many, many
avenues that we have left to cover in this our session
together. We have covered a lot on the subject of
healing, on the subject of healing the self and today
we would like to deviate just a little from this but we will say to
you that this is one of the main reasons we are creating this space
together.

We wish to discuss the fundamentals of your soul and the
soul's journey, from eon to eon, from ages to ages and to help
you to understand that you are not only a physical being in this
moment that you recognise but you are an energetic pattern of all
of the experiences that you have actually lived within the earth.
All of these experiences are alive and vibrating through you in
this moment but what is your spirit, what is the incarnational
process and why would you bother to even start the journey
from pure Divine Essence, perfection you might say, into this
less than perfect instrument that inhabits the earth? For what

purpose could this possibly have served? We would suggest that the service is to yourself, while you are on the earth you will go through two stages, these two stages shall be serving yourself and coming to an understanding of your own desires of what it is that makes you happy, self gratification, every aspect of the selfishness that you can possibly experience, you will have to walk through that door.

Through the very first incarnations that you will be placed upon the earth to inhabit and experience, this will be the prime force that will move you through the timeline of the life, it will be to receive for the self and to take what you feel you will never have enough of. The first part of this incarnational process will be to believe that you are totally and utterly a physical being living in this instant so therefore as you live in this instant you will have no concept of a brainwave that could suggest that if you do not consume all you will have some in reserve for another time. The primal force that we are talking about lives within the first three centres of the physical body, these first three centres work in harmony with the desire to receive totally for the self and for the self's own gratification. Now the self's own gratification is called that primal force, the survival instinct, it is encoded in this part of your body, it is the instinct that guides you through your life, even when you hit the higher altitudes of evolution that survival instinct will still be a very active part of the program.

It is important that you understand that there never comes a time when you do not have this primal force coursing and pulsating throughout the entire body, it is the governing, driving force that creates life and moves it forward for without this force being active within your being, you could not experience a physical life. So the soul does not have this aspect of the nature, the soul is perfect, the soul is luminous, the soul is weightless, the soul is timeless, the soul is like the aspect of the Sun's rays as it emanates and you see the ripple through time. From the time the Sun's rays leave the Sun's atmosphere to the time it is witnessed on the earth and transcends the upper stratosphere and into the atmosphere, you will understand that there is time in movement and motion forward, this is very much like the spirit.

The spirit governs the body but the spirit essence is held and contained within another stratosphere of the Divine element of your nature so we have just implemented two natures that run consecutively throughout your life. There is the primal force of the physical, the physical anatomy, the primal force of moving forward and survival instincts, there is the spirit essence and the timeless force, the weightless mass that is the movement instrument that pulls the strings and creates the cement, or the glue we will call it, that creates the body and spirit connection. The body and the spirit connection, although they are in consciousness coherent, they are still only two aspects of the whole, the third aspect that must be birthed into creation to create the incarnation, the physical expression, is the mindset. Now this is where we truly get to the battery source of all creation for without the mental field being placed into a working vibration between the spirit and the body, there is nothing that can be created, nothing that can be believed, nothing that can be experienced for it is the mind that must perceive the reality and it will be an individual reality. We would suggest to you that the individual reality will be based on how far along the evolutionary scale that the spirit has incarnated and lived along.

So we would suggest to you that although there is never a time when the spirit is not in connection with the higher source of its being, it cannot connect to the very essence of the physical being part of the experience until it has merged and worked its way into consciousness, the co-creative belief structures of the person's incarnation. Now these are the three elements that are absolutely fundamental, when you have an incarnation and the mind is not 100% in focus and in action and in alignment and fully present and fully working on its whole entirety at its highest potential, then you would have what you would call those who enter the earth with a disability, a brain dysfunction, this is chosen by that soul so that they will work within the other elements of their being. They will have to work with direct contact with the soul into physical form and the consciousness of the self is not birthed, however, for you the masses the consciousness of the self has to be fully present.

So if you could think of it like a three-pronged fork without all three ingredients, without all three points in total alignment and in total working harmony, there can be no physical incarnation. This is why it is so important to understand that without all of these elements, you cannot have new birth being born into the earth, and what about the spirit essence that we have been talking about, for there are many elements of the spirit. The spirit that we have been talking about is the impersonal spirit, that part of the spirit that is connected to the whole of creation, like the Sun warms the entire galaxy and yet there are individual aspects of your galaxy that the heat of the Sun touches and if you think of yourself as the individual aspect, you are the planet in the mix within the earth and within the cosmic makeup and the cosmic planning, the Universe as you have known it. So the spirit is like the Sun that warms and gives life to the individual aspect of the planet you would say, this individual planet, now this is where all of the relevant information is stored, the relevant information is then held in what we would call no less than an imprint, a blueprint, an individual aspect of that spark of the co-creative force.

Now as that aspect is then created and it decides that it will take physical form, the body is then created, remember that the body has one instinct and that is to survive, the mind has one function and that is to perceive the self and how the self relates to the world at large. This individual planet, this individual aspect will contain over many, many life experiences of the other two, over time, life, death – time, life, death, time between lives, life experience and death moving back to time between lives, all of the information is stored on the individual planet, that is that individual aspect of the entire self, the spirit, that is then connected up through those waves that are emitted from the Sun.

The planet is made up of those waves and your forces that bring that into creation and into a format is what you would call the gravitational pull, it is the magnet, it is the moment of creation when it becomes active.

When you take a picture and you place it in front of you, you can take a look at the overall picture or you can take a look at the individual brush strokes that created the picture, this is what your spirit has created, this is your spiritual life, your spiritual journey. As you work through this, you will have a great many lessons that you will have to endure, you would have to say "why is it then that life is so challenging?" Well, if you were to remain as part of the Source then you would have information at hand, as you move into the picture you can see that the pictures stands and creates a beautiful scene before your eyes, this beautiful scene before your eyes is an individual aspect of the entire strokes, the individual breakdown of the strokes of the pen, of the tapestry that is being created.

As you live each life you may think of it as another piece of that picture being placed into creation, once it has been created you would understand that it is now part of the whole picture, this is what your blueprint is. Now you have the language brought to the earth which has stated that you have seven energy centres within your body, you have one energy centre close to the body, this is the part that we are actually speaking of, this is that part that is active, this is that part that contains that picture. Think of the picture as being unfinished, think of the picture as in creation and in motion and always changing and every time that you have learned and brought one aspect to a close within the physical life, that picture then changes and the new picture is set to be built on, this is what you are doing – we would call this your universal fears, the part of the essence of the planet that is consecutively running through every individual aspect from the God force.

You truly are all gods in creation and yet you would not say that you are equal to God in power so how can this be? If you are God in motion in physical form, then why is it that you cannot access that higher power of the co-creative force that has created you? Well, it is truly simple, you have not built the framework of the picture yet, all of the parts that have not been finished and brought to finalisation cannot be imprinted on the blueprint, therefore how can you possibly expect to be in a space of knowing all, of creating all, of being a conscious part of the whole of creation? This is why you have, this is why you choose to undertake the experience of the incarnated, as you incarnate you are discovering the individual aspect contained within the whole of creation. The mental field truly is the understanding of the sense of self, it is your self in relation to the world in front of you, so this body that you call complete when born into the physical world you will understand, is but a snapshot of what it is that you have experienced to this point, what you will be has not been painted yet.

I would like you to really have a very long, hard think about the journey that you have taken from the time that you became aware of the sense of self and how you relate, how your place in the world was created, the life that you have built to house that aspect of your divinity. The primal force is only there to see that you have a vehicle with which to negotiate this part of your being, your spiritual, contractual life are the elements at force that bring all of the understanding through the mental field and that sense of individuation and separation so that you may experience the different fears, the different joys, the different aspects that the physical life will bring to you.

When all three are working in harmony, you have a body that is healthy and fit and strong, when you have a good sense of self, you have an ego that is strong and you have that sense of presence, when you have this then you have accessed how you view the events in the world and the relationships to you through the spiritual side of your nature. You will draw to you all of these experiences and people that will draw you ever closer to finishing the next stage in the picture. The spiritual side is the outside and external experience that you are participating in but it is not who you are and this is the essence of what it is that we are speaking to you about today.

You mistake this part of creation as your spirit and of who you are in relation to God and this is why you cannot find that God Source within – you have a popular belief that says "you are God" and yet you will not recognise this for you will continue to live these three aspects of your life and expect to see the Divine Creator manifest through these three personality aspects of the incarnational process. Who you are in the stream of life – you are the God force and yet not the force that you recognise, if you truly wish to see the God force within you, you will only access that when you can see beyond your physical life, the relationships that are presented, the experiences that you have gathered, the hurts and the emotional experiences that you have been participating in. The mind that tells you that you are an individual self and how you feel about that self, the survival instinct of the body to push you forward, to keep moving and creating a new part, a new aspect of the journey for until you have seen through this mirror then you can never, ever see the face of God within creation, you cannot come before the Father, Mother without having truly worked through all aspects of the physical part of your life.

You cannot understand what this Divine Creator truly is for your consciousness has not transcended that understanding of limitation of the three aspects of the physical construct that you have been living. As you start to transcend and as you start to truly understand why your life is in creation the way it has played out, you will do one thing, you will allow that life to totally consume you and you will create your hell upon earth in the lack of forgiveness and in anger and rage at what has been created which is what the mass has done. As you work through that level and you transcend to a more impersonal view of the cosmic plane, you will do one thing that will be different from the masses, you will look at the self and the experiences and you will remain unemotionally attached, you will stand in the light of acceptance.

If you truly want to understand the Divine Essence of God, understand acceptance, understand the total ability to have no attachments to any aspect of the three elements that you are most familiar with. As you work through this level, the world around you and the people who join you will look at you and think that you are heartless, you are devoid of emotion, you are spaced out in another vibration that we cannot accept for it is in that space of total acceptance and the complete release of your expectations of how you thought your life should be. When you truly meet this face of your soul and the journey, you will be moved to a place where every belief that you have ever placed any power of spirit or awareness into will completely be dismantled.

You will walk through the door of chaos and you will feel an insanity beyond description, do not fear this chaos for it is in the chaos that you are receiving the blessings of God for it is in the experience of the releasing of the weight of the soul's journey to this point, it is in the allowing of the dissolution of your expectations of yourself and of others, the surrender point where you will go through a process of death, rebirth and resurrection, three parts as you had with three physical aspects. You shall go through the three layers of the evolution and release of the weight of matter and you will be reborn into a belief pattern of union with the total cosmos and in that understanding, the resurrection, the ascension to a higher order of reality is now birthed into creation and into the three lower aspects of the personality and then you have Christ on earth for without this resurrection and acceptance and awareness of expectation and surrender and death of all false beliefs and false gods, you cannot stand before the Light of the Creator. You have called this alchemy where you have merged the light and the dark and in that moment spontaneous combustion of energy and light is radiated through the physical being and then healing can be directed through and channelled out into the earth. When that person walks through a door or into a village or in time, the whole of the surroundings will move in to that vibration and light that the being is emanating and all of the souls that are ready to follow that level of awareness and Divine Majesty shall follow that process and that person on earth.

We have said before that the essence of the Christ has been born on your earth at this point, you are looking for a God, you are looking for that aspect of the Light and you expect nothing short of miracles and this is again the expectations that you are being asked to place before your feet and to bow down in awareness and humble servitude to the Divine aspect of that being even though they may take a very physical form.

We have been wishing to share this aspect of maturation into the higher altitude of the spirit, the light that we said has come from the Sun, we would say that this is being birthed into the earth and has been for some time. We have placed prophets upon the earth to foretell and to breathe this consciousness and create a new language within the earth and the global consciousness, the global dream of accepted reality - we are now introducing that light as the ninth centre of reality. Where we said that you have the seven centres within the body and the eighth above, the ninth centre is the centre of your galaxy, of your Milky Way, it is the centre point from where all of creation emanates and it is the smallest point in the Universe and at the same time the paradox is that it is the entire Universe of your galaxy and Milky Way. All of creation is birthed from this point, you have called it the Big Bang, and we call it Spirit, the soul lives in the eighth centre of your reality, the experience lives in the seven memory reactor chips.

Torus energy is the vibrational magnet which keeps all of life flowing harmoniously for you and life force in motion, not unlike the gravitational pull around the planet, this is the life force that you are emitting, the battery cells that keep the body healthy. It has been said that it can be placed around and measured out but it cannot be truly measured by any instrument upon the earth, this is the field that influences the world around you. When you go out into nature, this is the field that alerts the plants to your presence, the animals, you speak to the animals through this energy that you emit. If you are walking through life in anger, resentment, feeling sad, this is what your animal kingdom, nature spirits, plants and Mother Earth shall inherently feel emanating from you, it is in your best interests to look at the emotional information that is concealed between the seven centres of the physical energy field and to re-look at where you have placed these emotional charges that are being emitted. All of this happens in every second of the experience in physical form from the moment that you are born on the earth, this is in motion in every second and you are painting the picture, stroke by stroke, using the eighth centre to align through this tutorous energy field, the experiences which will continue to move you forward and this is why you have had such a strong pull to survival instinct.

Comfort, greed and profit over all others and the reality of "the world is a competitive dog eat dog reality" was born when in actual fact it is in complete harmony with all of life that you find the most peace and that is when the world will be created in the image of the Garden of Eden as you have come to understand it. You will come from Source and you will return home to Source and you will be ready to realign and continue with the sojourn and the experiences within the life, this is the blessing; this is the absolute perfection that you are.

We ask you to have reverence for the majestic beauty that is in creation in every aspect of your life.

Do you have any questions?

We thank you for the information brought through today and we will leave any questions for another time.

We thank you for your patience, we have met before, you have known me as Paul, and I thank you for your love and attention this day, God bless.

12 - BARTHOLOMEW – NOVEMBER 20, 2008

*... We must ask you to ponder the magnificence
of life for you have separated life and living and
death and dying and the reality is that you are in
either part of that process...*

Greetings – it is indeed a pleasure to be with you this afternoon, it is Bartholomew Benedictine at your pleasure sir and madam and welcome to you both.

It is indeed a rare pleasure to be able to commune with those in your realm, we look forward to conversing with you, indeed I do enjoy the communion that we hold, it is rather sacred and this is what we will talk about, sacredness - the mystical eye of the journey of sacredness, the sacred heart, establishing your temple, establishing your reality within the fabric of that spiritual journey that you all undertake when you agreed to participate in the dance of creation from non-substance, thought, energy, light and motion to depth, weight, density into manifestation. We love the process and you are either in one process or another as you already know, you are either in the process of living or in the process of passing and living on the other side of your reality. Either way we could say that it is a cycle, either way from which ever lens you choose to view it from, in our realm you are still living and you are still transcending that place of the earth into the spirit and you are transcending that place of the spirit into the earth.

We must ask you to ponder the magnificence of life for you have separated life and living and death and dying and the reality is that you are in either part of that process, the life that is too fearful to live and the process of death and the releasing back into life. It is a magical journey and it is mystical and the sadness on our side of life is that you do not seem to wish to sit and to ponder the magnificence of the process. We fear that you think that you can outrun this process, perhaps you just take it for granted, it does not matter, it is a process nonetheless and when the time is right your life will call upon you to make that journey into the mystical aspect of your nature for you are all mystical and you are all mystics, you have merely forgotten.

So we would say to you that as you traverse this life, as you breathe your life on the earth, pay homage to the process for it is a magical process that has taken a very long period of linear time to build, evolve and grow and this is the process of life and living but where do you start the journey what is the point, the individual spark born that decides to begin the process and do you do this randomly or do you do this as a evolution in the process of enlightenment? We believe that there is an analogy – from the light of the light and the dark of the dark, from the hellish depths of the void to the magical lightness and brightness of maturation and this is where you are at any given time. We say that this is the map, it is complete and it is ever evolving, there will never be a time when you are not negotiating this map but what is this map, what is the essence of the map for that is the essence of life, the essence of your spiritual journey, it is not you for who you are you could not comprehend but it is the essence of the journey.

So we take you back to the point of separation but there is no separation – we will call your spirit the ocean, the tide, the flow of energy, the wave and the particle, you are the stream, you are this wave, you are this particle of this ocean, of this movement of this kinetic energy field and you are content and you are complete and you are in a place of complete awareness of all, of instantaneousness, of supremacy of the journey and the magic of your own essence, you are the living memory of everything that has ever been created and the extreme ecstasy of every moment of that experience – you are, there is nothing that you can describe to compare with what you are in this state. You are everything that has ever formed, you are the breath of the wind and you exist in the pool of timelessness, there is no moving forward, there is no releasing past, there is just the majesty of the entirety and you are that, you call it eternal, you call it God, you call it Light, we call it Source. We only call it Source because we have to put it into a language but it is not a language, it can never be spoken, it is a frequency, it is a speed and a note, it is an octave, you are that sound, that vibration.

If you were to pluck the string of a guitar, you do not see the note but you hear the pitch and it is sound and it is music to your ears, dear ones this is what you are, so why on earth would you begin a process that will take eons of time and move into separation and that light of the light, that octave and that note separates, we come back to the ocean of God and we say "brother, sister it is time to experience the separation and to descend into density and darkness" and so we create the drop in its perfection and form, it contains the whole of the essence of the ocean yet the mass and the construct is of a separate dimension and with the breath of the All and the Almighty, we breathe you into the birthing process. You must drink from that river and forget who you are, you must feel the feeling of aloneness, of separation, of darkness, of being abandoned by the whole of who you are and being left alone to conceive of a world of your own construct.

When we view a child, it is warm and radiant when the eyes meet with the protector and the loving warmth of the parental vibration but in that instant when that parent is removed and that child cannot feel and sense and see that protection, it feels vulnerable, the fright and fear resonates in the note of its creation and reality and the signals of the intuition and of the bodily system that govern, ignite and spark into anxiety and fear. It sets a chemical response, a system that builds within systems all flowing, this is where you find yourself, this is what you would call the pits of hell for it is not evil neither has it ever been malevolent, it has merely been the construct of separation and the universal fears. The whole point of the separation is in the embracing of the fears and it is that emotive response that you are here to master, to experience and to mature back to the springs of eternity.

So you take this journey and you move from separation into a physical life, into weight and you become that vulnerable child and the father image of your God on earth was born from within your very cells and this was the dynamic that brought that perception into creation. As you have all risen from the ocean of eternity, we shall call it, into the river and the droplet of separation you all resonate these fears and vulnerability, they are what you remember, they are the essence, they are the driving force for your physical body is a mere reflection of this emotion that you have ignited in the separation.

So the tribal force, the force field and the magnetics that emanate from every individual spark is the understanding that they need to connect with the individualisation of that ocean and they recognise that in the partnerships and the friendships and those who come to join them on the journey. They magnetically draw into each other's orbit exactly what they need in this process of life so soul groupings are birthed into creation and you live this creation over and over.

We have been dropping a perception into the instrument's consciousness for we wished her to understand that as the eons of time, as the motion of life draws forward and moves you from one time into a new time, it is the same souls, it is the same groupings that recommence, that rejoin, that re-vibrate in harmony and play the tune of life. It is those experiences that move you through time, from one time, from one life, from one experience, from one thought to one emotion. This is the glue, each part of the whole, each part of the individual aspect, the brick in the wall and as you move forward you map the history of this individual experience and it goes down in history, it is prophesised, it is made into text, it is memorised, it is spoken but it is never forgotten for it is who you are and it is as much a part of the life that you live in the next time as it was in the previous time for that is the foundation of who you are in that moment of life.

As you remember the past you become aware that you were that civilisation, that you are that tribe, that there was never a time when that life left your field of experience, you just did not bring it into the consciousness of the moment through the memory of experience but it is the reaction point of what it is that is happening, it is the event of the life that you are looking at today that is built from the memories of the distant past and of who you were in that life.

We are introducing you fully to your spiritual body, you have worked through the scientifics of the DNA, of the blood and the bone and the meat structure of your life, you have looked at the emotive responses and reactions, you have looked at the beliefs and the creation of that reality and now we introduce you, not for the first time for we continually retouch on all the areas that we have already brought forth, to the spiritual body of your being, to the construct of your life. For what purpose was I placed upon the earth? – this is a question that is longer than time, older than time, it is the golden thread that links every incarnation and physical experience and every non-physical and between incarnations, this is the thread of your life, this is the question that drives you forward, this is the unanswered question.

So you say to each other "when I am born, I know one thing with any surety, it is that my time on earth for this life will draw to an end and when I move on to this life between lives I will contact those still living the earth life to awaken them to the possibility that they are far more than the limitation that they have experienced in that life and as I make that link, it is that thread of what purpose we are born and there must be more to this life than I know". It is in the question, that is the mystery, which is the mystical experience for that understanding, that little piece of dissatisfaction, the unanswered questions, for this is truly the essence that spurs you on and as you push forward, you are in a constant process of awakening that next level of understanding.

So we meet from our side with you from your side and we bring with us the memories and the knowing of that pool of reality, that Divine Source that you are and we stand and we guard and we nurture and we seek to heal the illusions and the fears that have woven themselves into the tapestry of the incarnational process. We are the guardians of the pool and we will not move and ascend into the pool until all of the fears and the separation have melted away and the individual droplet of the essence of the ocean, that pool of water, has returned back and merged. Now this will truly be the Garden of Eden for it was when you left the majesty of the ocean and the pool of all the fears reflected in the separation that you became physical in form and the promised land is the merging and the melting away of boundaries and separation and the drying up of the pool of the fears of the individual, of the soul groupings and then the droplet, the individual returns to the ocean and adds all of the wisdom, all of the mastery of individualisation.

It is in the losing of the self for it is in the birth of self-awareness that you choose to incarnate and start the process and it takes you into ego, into selfishness, self-awareness, seeking only to serve the self and the self needs into the selfless, into the releasing and the needing of any and all external sources and the emerging as the selfless, humble servant of mankind. That individual drop loses its sense of self, the power of compassion, you will melt into the eye of the heart for the true selfless person who has come through separation and fear and has merged with the awareness of eternity and essence for they see no boundaries, they tear down structure and they view their fellow man from their heart, they feel love, they sense inescapable service to the fellow beings within their consciousness. As they lose that sense of self and boundaries and strip away need, their heart is left bare and they love for the sake of love, they give for the burning desire to be of selfless service, they give and need not receive, they are illuminated and enlightened and the heart of compassion, they cry for the pain of another for that pain is as real to them for they know no separateness.

This is where you move into becoming the droplet being released back into the ocean and here lies the paradox – for you never love the individual sense of your own construct, your individuality, however, you are not separate, you are connected and the ocean of the God force runs through every part of that drop of individuality and that is what creates God on earth. You do not necessarily have to go back and become selflessly lost in the ocean of eternity, you may elect to be used as an instrument so pure, so selfless to help bridge and to help cross the illusions of those fears that you once were blinded by.

Your Buddha on the earth followed this process, you wrote down his illuminated life, the bridge from physical reality and individual self to essence and selfless and enlightened. The awakening of the heart and the mind and the perception and the clear sight and wisdom to view the world and see the illusions and sit in the enlightenment of compassion and love for we have said before that you are born of the earth, you who are the highest of the high, the lightest of the light, the lowest of the low, the darkest of the dark – this is the contract, the continuum, the golden path, the thread, this is the journey of ascension into mastery and you are all living the experience and the construct of where that individual experience and to what degree you have mastered the fears, separateness and illusions as to where you are on the continuum of the evolution into mastery. It is so rare that one attains that level of mastery, enlightenment and then returns to the earth that you create religions, philosophies, stories and fictions about those lives on earth.

Think of the brightness of the teachings and the essence of compassion that these entities bring in on that one incarnation for their wisdom transcends your lifetime and is contained throughout the eons into a new time and you build and construct your roads of ascension basing the teachings on the teachings and awareness of those masters.

I spent lifetime after lifetime in the depths of the belief and illusions of that web of creation and fiction within monasteries and spent lifetime after lifetime writing, scribing and dictating these myths. From my side as I sit in this very moment, I assure you, this was as much a falsehood and an illusion as any illusion can be. In the freedom of living, in the power of choice I worked this life, I continued to live it and to be blinded until the ascension over many lifetimes brought me to disillusionment for this is where the spiritual essence of illumination lies in the darkest night of your soul and the breaking down of all of the illusionary systems, this is where the light becomes illuminated.

Through this ascension you are now ready to receive a new version of a truth but it is only a truth in as much as you can accept that level and as the time comes you will again break down the blinders and find yourself in the shedding of the falseness of the illusions and the fears to transcend to a higher version of that truth. You will not complete the journey on the earth for that would not be possible, think of the earth as a kindergarten taking care of you younger souls at the point where the physical life, the tree of life can no longer serve the maturation, you will make that choice to ascend to the keepers of the pool of the fears and the separation for all the tears of despair are gathered in this pool and you will be its gate keepers, its guardians, its door keepers and you will start the next part of the incarnational process and you will work in union with the younger souls, not unlike the parent nurturing and protecting its child. As you work through all of the aspects that this part of the journey brings, you will again find yourself at the crossroad into the ocean.

The masters have taken that step, they are the keepers of certain times of the earth where the essence of their teachings held the fabric of the beliefs of the masses and as nothing is ever lost, forgotten, that time is still relevant and is still active in your journey into the spiritual body of your being because you, dear friends, are the people who inhabited that master's consciousness. So we say that the masters have their own plane of energy that you may and can and will emote and you will connect and depending on which lifetime you spent working with the masters will depend on the masters who you are drawn to the strongest. The master of this time is the Christ energy and so when this energy falls in to memory and the new master's teachings have breathed consciousness and movement away from that Master Christ energy, there will be those who will look at the images and the crosses and all of that fabric that created that time and be drawn to that energy – no different than the master Melchizedek, the master Lanto, the masters who have been and who are still contained within your memory.

You are not individual, you are an aspect of the whole and as you experience individuality, that is the gift of life. The New Age birthed and in process, the three hundred year window moving out of the old age and the three hundred year window moving through into the New Age, you will understand that is the bridge – this is the construct of your experience, this is the construct of the yugas, this is that philosophy and where it was birthed into your reality and are you moving into a Golden Age, why would you repeat an age that has been experienced? We would suggest that there will be a New Age but it will not be based in one area of a past paradigm, it will be the construct of all of the paradigms of the evolution of the chain and the New Age will be a product, an amalgamation of all that has gone before and a new master shall govern that and that is the belief that you create your own reality and that will be the essence of the construct of the future possibilities and it is being birthed and given substance and belief in this very instant. You will not know the master, you will not expect the master and we smile for we see the master and we know the teachings, we give you the teachings for that is the birth of the New Age and this Age shall be holographic, fractile, that Age shall breathe that if there is one part created, then every part of creation shall be a representative and reflection of that fractile image, it is geometric, it is mathematical and it is perfect in its nature. Linear weight and time will be relative to the understanding of the quantum holograph of reality, it is in essence in every part of you and of every part of the world and the globe and the Universe.

The Universe is created by rays of light and this ray of light that we have given you in past sessions; it is the ray of light known as the Blue Ray. The Blue Ray vibrates peace, transcendent of time, translucent in nature; all the laws of your physics shall be shattered as you awaken the power of the fractile image. The fractile image and beliefs were born into your earth some three hundred years ago but could not be proven nor substantiated but the very essence of its creation and conception was the very essence of the fractile image because one conscious being could conceive, perceive an idea of whatever is created is a part of a mathematical picture and in every aspect is created in the same image moving through the magnetics into the smallest component, cell and construct. Once that was created, that belief, that possibility, then it was merely a matter of linear time and maturation and fine tuning and creating new systems to work within the map of reality.

Now you can truly understand the fractile image, the reflection of the self, the snowflake is totally representative of the individual aspect of water, it is a part of the frozen moisture and if you take one part of that flake, all the other parts will morph to reflect that change – this is the Blue Ray, the red laser, x-ray was built and formatted in the Saturn, red heat of passion and earth and fire. We birth the cool, calm ocean of the Blue Ray, the quantum holograph, if one can conceive it is there for all to experience.

You have been trying to understand where the earth is moving and we are working to bring this understanding. If this is reflective of a holographic consciousness then you individually, atom by atom, cell by cell, protein by protein, amino acid by amino acid, you are the building blocks that reflect the quantum hologram and so just looking at another you are already experiencing this New Age, it has always been with you but you have not had the consciousness to understand and perceive which is the essence of this teaching that there is never anything that has been created that can ever be lost – it is just that you have not ascended to that reality.

So we pose a question to you – how do you know that the reality of your life is truly representative of reality and how do you know what is truth, real, it is only that you can accept that picture and construct it and believe its reality and so when you sit on the chair, it feels solid but is it solid? You now know that it is not but your density is a vibrational match in speed which is light and so the two meet on that level of reality – but is the chair solid and are you solid? From our side of life that is a reflective question for when you can truly see the truth of that answer, you will walk through a dark night like no other, now this is when you can connect with the wormholes you have named them and move through time. When you can ascend to that level of truth and reality, you shall meet the neighbours, you shall blend with a new level and the neighbours are not extra-terrestrial, they are you, they are us.

We have given you much to ponder, your guardians and door-keepers who you so fondly interact with are mere links in a chain and they are guarding and protecting, as a parent, your mythologies and beliefs and the tears of disillusionment and separation that you have shed and they shall stay with you until that pool reflects the new order of reality from separation into enlightenment and completeness.

We bid you farewell and we say to you that your temporal form is an instrument to serve your life, use the instrument wisely, think of it as a temple, think of it as the spiritual chamber of your reality, build on silence, create sacred space, revere the mystery and allow illumination to filter through these inner chambers and create the building that you can retire into to take breath from the reality of your life.

Your body is the temple of your life, honour that part of your essence and we bid you adieu and farewell to you dear friends.

13 - KUKUWANI –
DECEMBER 5, 2008

*...the spirit and the nature kingdom, about the
elementals that live within the earth...*

 We will speak to you this evening about the spirit
and the nature kingdom, about the elementals that
live within the earth but first of all, may I say it is
indeed a very exciting time for me personally for
I have the opportunity to present myself to you
this evening.

We on the spirit side of life are very adaptable and we are happy
to fit in to your busy schedules. As you know we are never far
from you, we are always walking with you and we are guiding you
but we would like to bring in the different levels of consciousness.
We have spent a great many months speaking of the consciousness
of humanity, humanity is the only consciousness that is self-aware,
making the self aware of its presence is purely intelligence, that is
not to say that the other realms do not have intelligence for they
do, however, it is the awareness of the individual, now that is a
higher consciousness than the other realms.

The other realms that govern the other life forces and we
will say as a disclaimer that all of the earth is a life force, it is all
a vibrational frequency emitting and omitting life but within

that sphere there are many layers, there is the human life and the human construct which is in essence complicated and complex, creative in its design, it is like a rug that is hand-woven, thread by thread, each thread feeding through the crossing threads and it makes a pattern but the pattern builds, the pattern grows and becomes more complex as that pattern grows. The availability of that intelligence, the comfortableness and the recognition of the patterns that you are living, the ease that you slip into those patterns, the awareness that you have about those patterns, that is the experience of consciousness and of life.

So when we use the terminology of the Divine tapestry, that is in essence what is always meant and we wish to share with you that each thread in the pattern is an individual experience that has been lived and breathed and brought into creation. You have many different layers within this and we shall bring you to the animal kingdom, we shall bring you to a consciousness which has no sense of separation, it is fully a part of the tapestry and the individuation only occurs on the physical, on the physical realm of the human experience and yet you are surrounded by the nature kingdom.

Think of all of the threads that go into this tapestry, they are all united but within the human experience it is relevant to you the individual whereas from the animal kingdom it is relevant to the whole of creation, they are born aware of the higher self at the time of the physical birth, they do not forget what is the nature, the natural order, what is the natural order? Why is it that a baby being born can immediately stand? It is because it needs to protect and to move with the herd, this is the natural order, this is the creation and this is the inseparableness of that kingdom. What separates the two realms? That of the physical and that of the animal kingdom in the physical, it is merely speed, it is a speed of light, it is the movement of time and it is divine in nature.

I have been one of those Shamans who lived and worked and spoke with the animal kingdom, I have also spoken to the nature kingdom for as much as we can acknowledge that the great spirit of the animal is alive, we do not see the kingdom of nature in the same light for we do not feel the warmth of the body or the breath or the heart pumping for all of that is contained in the marvel of the inner circuitry of that creation and yet alive the plants are. They breathe as you breathe but they breathe through the surface of the leaves, of the flowers, of the stalks and of the root structure. It is the same pattern as the animals as they breathe the oxygen through the nostrils, as the human inhales where the animal does it involuntarily and on a natural cycle for it is completely contained within the Great Spirit of that cycle, of that memory, of that connection, of that inseparableness. The human can use the breath and can actually curtail the breath, decide how deep the breath shall be, shall I breathe through my stomach or shall I breathe shallow in my chest, shall I hold my breath or do I breathe rapidly.

Now the human is conscious that he has control over the breath, the animal kingdom, they are aware that the breath is the essence of life and it is involuntary, it is automatic and they do not see the need to control the breath. The plants, they do not breathe through a nostril, they absorb through the surface, they draw in and they take the nutrients from that and it is dispersed but it is still patterned on the animal and the human for there is a vascular system that is the circuitry of the mass of the vegetation, no different from the organs and the construct of your physical bodies.

When you truly understand the three elements that we have spoken about, then you can access that energy and you can speak the language of that level of consciousness but there is still another realm and this realm is denser than that of the nature kingdom, the animal kingdom and the human kingdom and that is the element of the soil, of the rocks, that is denseness, it is weight, it is pure carbon that has fossilised and it has changed in its elemental composition, it is in creation God's food for without the minerals that are created in that fossilisation of the nutrients, the individual building blocks, there could be no life for the plants would have nothing to sink its roots into and to feed upon.

So if we were to look at the elemental kingdom in the scheme of the planet and of life, that is the core essence, that is the structure that is of the utmost importance and yet time and time throughout history it is that force that you strip and that you show no reverence for. You do not even stop to acknowledge this but that is the source of your lives for without it there could be no breath for any of the other three systems to live, to breathe, there could be no existence, this is the glue and it is as ancient as ancient and when we work with the healing of the body, when we speak to the spirit of the animal that has sacrificed its life force to sustain us, it is a supreme act, it is in essence the supreme act of the elemental earth in the sustenance, in the creation of life.

So as a tribe it is only natural that you would be a part of all of those systems and that if you had the consciousness, if you had the awareness of your majestic individual self, then it is only natural that you have the same expression within the animal kingdom, therefore when the animal gives its life for you, you give your life to the animal which in turn is returned to the elements for the vegetation to continue the sustenance, it is a cycle, it is what is known as the great rhythmic cycle, the drum, the rolling of time and of essence. We use all of the elements and we draw from the pool of creation and life and as we feel the life that has sacrificed, it can never be heard through the physical senses for this is not possible, it will be heard as a frequency, a feeling in your heart and in your very body.

You all know those feelings of gratitude, of warmth, of love, that is the language of that kingdom and when you open to that vocabulary, you can speak to all of creation, there are no limits to what you can hear. Your animals are your guides, they are your accompaniment through life, they are your best friends and they are also playing the role of the offender, there are times and rhythms and cycles in the Great Spirit of life. When you see yourself as the Great Spirit, when you look into the eyes of your companions, you will understand that they are your equal and that they are there in service to you for they have a natural awareness of selflessness tempered with basic primal survival instinct. They do no try to hide it, they do not feel that they are above it, they are at one, they can communicate that oneness, they have a gift more precious than your jewels and that is the gift of selflessness, of humility before the Great Spirit of life, each with its linking arms cascade through the eons of time and your very existence is aware and linked to this connection for the animals eat of the vegetable kingdom as you do, the vegetable kingdom, the plants, they are your cabinets of medicine, they are your fabric of building blocks, they are perfect and take selflessness and existence and timelessness into a higher dimension.

You see them as inanimate, unfeeling, unaware and yet on the higher vibration they are absolutely animate, they are always in motion, they are always creating and modifying their own structure, they are more evolved than the human structure has ever been for they can create from their very essence the fruits, the seeds, the entirety of the sustainability of all of the life forms that live in union with them, you humans see yourselves as superior. When a flower is cut without permission, it is a violation against that perfect creation, when a tree is fallen and cut up to serve your needs, it cries tears, the sap oozes and trickles from within its core.

When you understand the majestic beauty and can see through the door of the higher realm, the higher dimensional pull, you could not violate a life form in this manner. If you hold the trunk of the tree, you will feel eternity within its fabric and now we come to man and we challenge man for there is no other elemental kingdom, vegetation, animal that so purposely affects justice and extracts revenge so cold and calculating.

If you were to look at the carnage that has been lived within the earth in the last weeks of your experience *(we felt that this remark referred to recent terrorist attacks in India)*, ask yourself this question – when your fellow brothers fell and you bore witness to that atrocity, did you weep with sorrow as if he was your brother, if he were to pass in that manner, your mother or your father of the earth, or did you view that as a separateness that was tragic but yet has not affected your life personally? When the ones who are responsible have been tracked down with vengeance, do we then take their lives to please own our sense of injustice and is that justice served? The hypocrisy, the hands in the air, the anger and the outrage and we say to you as the Great Spirit, not a single flame or spark but as a Great Spirit of humanity, if one has been cut down, do you weep for that soul? You are that soul and you can speak to that spirit, it would tell you - do not be angry, do not be vengeful, pray a prayer of gratitude for the love that has been shared, the experience that has been played upon the earth, for the availability of all of the factors in the tapestry to have been made available for each entity to work with each other in the creation of the picture within the tapestry, within the threads being threaded together for when you truly understand the Great Spirit, there is only perfection. It is only when you stand in separation and judgment that you feel victimised, that you extract vengeance, this vengeance is venom and it pulses through the very veins of your own body.

So we say to you that those who perpetrated, those who were victimised and fallen, they are crying for you, for you do not understand the agreements and the celebration that is being experienced in that moment. When you live in anger, you cannot find peace; the door that will open in peace will come only through gratitude and understanding, releasing of your individual feelings and celebrating the unity of all of the different elements that are being played out upon your earth.

We knew this, our tribe of elders taught this sacred wisdom to our children, we were in harmony with the great elements of the earth, the element, the elemental, the vegetable, the animal and of course the celebration of humanity. You are divine but you are not above that rock that you simply step on to get to what you want. Wisdom is knowing that as you step on the rock to get you over to the other side of the river with dry feet that the rock has been placed there to serve you and so to thank, to live in that moment of gratitude, this is eternal wisdom and when you can truly live with this Divine Intelligence pulsating through every cell and every breath, you could never wilfully cause harm, make judgment on any part of creation for it is ignorance that gives birth to that and that is anger and separateness.

All of the teachings that you will ever hear throughout the whole of the earth that come from that Divine Intelligence will teach you this, it is simplicity, it is the simplest concept ever birthed, it is you who complicate it. We urge you to come before the face of God, this simple truth must pulse in every beat of the heart, be expressed in every breath that you take, be lived in every moment of your lives for only then can you stand before the face of your Creator, that essence of all that you see before you and all that was created to accompany you and sustain you.

Your biblical truth is this simplicity and this fact.

We will ask you if there are any questions that you wish to ask us.

(See Questions and Answers)

We thank you for your respect and your attention and we would give you, for you do not know who is speaking to you, but we would give you our love and our blessings and our hand in brotherhood and we will bid you farewell.

14 - WINSTON WHITEHORSE – DECEMBER 18, 2008

*...the laws of karma, cause and effect, like attracts
like, action and reaction, the fundamental
structure of thy Universe...*

A poet I am by my very nature and I feel that what we will be discussing today will be poetry to thy ears. Let us discuss the laws of karma, cause and effect, like attracts like, action and reaction, the fundamental structure of thy Universe, the fundamental structure of thy life, the fundamental structures of the mental field for it is through what you believe that you will first embrace the law of karma.

Winston Whitehorse was my name and I was a scribe in the 16th Century, I lived in a little town near Norfolk in the British Isles but you would have known it in that day as Brittany. There was quite an invasion at that time, for many years on and off we had been having the heathens from the other country, the more Germanic nations as you would know them and they would come in, and this was random bursts and they would take over the land and they were very vicious, they were very vicious in the sense that they were true warriors and they would maim so we had to very much fall into line. People do not understand that the Britain that they know today is more reflective of the Germanic culture than of the Celtic cultures and of the Northumberland cultures and the Norfolk country areas and the different areas that were lying around the rambling hills of that place, that country.

To me it is like a tapestry, it is like a quilt and it is mixed up with many, many dialects and many, many sub-cultures and the Germanic really brought more of a harmonic blend to the natural areas as opposed to the little infrastructures that had been set up, you would perhaps think of them as enclaves, the clan culture and mentality, so there was quite a shift in that perception. There is a reason that we are giving you this history lesson and that is because we very much wish to look at the karmic energies of the two nations, the German nation and the British nation. Both of them are built on war, both of them are militarised construct, they both had royalty, they both had society and a lot of that royalty was intertwined as we moved through the generations and the centuries and as we all know this is what was done politically.

When we are thinking of karma, we often limit it to the concept that if I take an action from you and against you, then that action is what you will be met with but this is not the true essence of the karmic energy and the karmic ties. The true energy of karmic ties would suggest that as you vibrate a belief, as you live that belief, as you act upon that belief, then that is the energy that is being set up and brought into physicality, it is the essence of what it is that is preceding you, it is preceding you because the energy is always moving, it is always moving fluidly, it is always moving forward by your standards of time. Karma is really just forward moving time, it is a time and place that you have not yet caught up with but yet you set the seeds in a previous state of consciousness.

So again we come back to the German culture and the British culture, now the German culture was at its peak and at its strength through your German, through your Nazi associations and socialism. The British responded in kind to this threat which they perceived to be worldwide, so the two countries went to war, but if you understood, the world war that you perceived on the earth had already been set in motion a long time ago for again there was that karmic connection throughout the centuries. When we said that through the Germanic cultures they randomly in their mode of transport entered onto foreign land and took that land for their own and maimed and subdued and brought in their own culture, it is interesting to think that the British culture has a very strong connection to the Germanic culture which is what is the basic foundation of modern Brittany, modern, we are not talking about the Dark Age Brittany, we are talking about modern Brittany, it was based on that foundation.

How very interesting that when we connect the two cultures, they again meet each other in war and it is again the perceived threat, this time it is not through the Danish and through that endeavour, it is more through the actual German nation itself, it is more home based but do you not think that William the Conqueror could not have come in just in one lifetime to be such a mighty ruler and warrior and not come back and also experience the other side of that, so who would that be – we would suggest that you may find it would be Goering, we think you would know him as Hermann Goering and they would come back and again they would seek to conquer and they would again look to create the war machine that was created from the past. The leaders of the British nations would again merge to meet that threat and to meet that energy of destruction, so the karmic wheel was cast and the die was set generations before the century that it was to replay out in for the memories of the cultures are long lived. Again we must say that there is always another proceeding that and that was the assassination of the Emperor and in that assassination attempt the Germans felt that they had lost face, their culture had come to a standstill, they went into complete crises and then that die was cast and again that leader shall be set forth to give birth to a new nation and to go in and rebuild that nation, then take that nation to its superior outcome which was set in motion generations before.

This is how karma, on a global construct, on a nation to nation, on a universal and contractual agreement from countries, a global consciousness can be playing out but again we will say one element of karma only for as many levels as you can imagine as to the depth of the karmic ties for this is the masses and the pool of the energy on the earth, the belief structures, nation and country and it will always have a karmic link. There can never be two nations that meet that are not karmically linked and there is always a thread that runs through from times gone by to present time, it cannot be other.

Now let us take it down to the karmic links of the soul group, the individuals who make up the culture and again we come down to a misperception and this misperception says to you that if I take action against you, then that action shall be met in my life, like attracts like. So we have a code of conduct that is birthed into the earth, take no more than what is taken but if an eye is taken, then take an eye, we have this getting even, we have the energy of revenge, we have the energy of vengeance and for a long time the individual karmic pool from person to person has been playing out along that thread – would you not agree? If I take an action against one, I would need to take an action and expect that action to be returned to me but we would say to you that this is absolutely like a newborn baby's view of karma and it is played out in that vibration. A far deeper version of this, or truth of this, is that it is **not that the action** that you take, it is not the person you are perceived to have hurt but it is more along the line of **the intention** with which the act was perpetrated.

You see, you can go over and slap someone's face and that slap will hurt that person physically but if you have the intention of waking them up when they were in danger, then that would be perceived as an act of service. However, if that person was just sleeping and you went over and slapped their face, then that person would perceive that as an attack, either way, where do you think the action point would be reverberated back to you? Does that mean that because you have slapped someone's face that they will slap you back, that you will be sitting and someone will come up to you and slap you? Do you not see that it is a very childish notion of karma, that karma runs so much deeper and through so many levels of your being, do you not realise that without karma you could not possibly be on the earth at this time? We do not call it karma, we call is the law of action and reaction, intention and expression and intention and expression is a far different energy from the law of cause and effect and the level that we have been speaking about.

Now that we have introduced you to the concept of global karma, nation upon nation, for that is valid and that is certainly playing out as a part of the tapestry of the earth, it is not individually received but it is an action and reactive on that level, it is so but the level that we want to talk about today is that intimate level that goes far deeper into your soul and this is how we would like to explain it to you.

We will walk into the place before your birth, you have moved from earth having had a rich life, you are now in a place between the worlds, you are not fully of spirit, you are not fully of earth, you are in a transitionary state, your connection to earth is weakening and it is fading and your emergence into spirit, well that is becoming more strengthened and it is like a pull and it is drawing you near. As you move into this state and you become more sensitive, you become aware of where it is that you are sitting and we will say it is sitting for we have no other words to describe as you hover in spirit, as you emanate, as you vibrate, whichever words you like but you are present and you become aware of that separation. The world that you have left is still very real to you and you know that you are going back because you feel that in every part of your circuits that are coming back to life but not at this moment, not at this second in time, you emanate.

You will not meet a judge, you will not meet the lords of karma for it has been said on your earth that there will be individuals very much like the judicial system that you have and they will then replay and reflect on your life and judge you on how well you fared. We will say to you that this is garbage, it is absolute nonsense, you will not meet the panel of experts so to speak, the lords of karma but you will meet Essence, you will meet your own Essence, you will meet the energy of all of the lives that you have lived before, think of it like this – if one area of your life with a relationship and partnership has been played out on the earth, then the relationship/partnership that mirrored the lifetime previous setting up that construct, well that energy will meet you in the next life, the life between lives and in that moment it will bring with it the expansive knowledge of every time that particular energetic connection has been re-experienced and re-negotiated. With that all of the ripples through the life just led, through the life just experienced, will then be reviewed in front of you and then the energy of the life lived and experienced prior to that will meet that energy and it will be like a sliding scale, how far along that reaction, that experience have you moved, did you move forward, did you do it better, did you manage to bring peace to that particular experience, did you mature it, how did you respond in that moment? When that person was driving you nuts did you slap their face with the intention of hurting them or did you turn the other cheek, what was it? Then in relation the ripple will then show you the relation of the previous experience and the previous experience and the previous experience and in that moment you will get that entire download, we will put it in computer terms for you, that entire download - then you get a sense of exactly where it is that you are on that time scale continuum.

Interestingly enough, it will almost be like a register of "oh! I could have done better, not quite matured, not quite finished, let's re-look at that in the next life" – right, that's done, organised and sealed, contract agreement, done. Now the next part, remember that the Universe is limitless and expansive and so in this instant you are doing this with all the different areas that you have been living, this is the true essence of karma, it has nothing to do with what you are doing in that moment, there will be no one coming in to judge you, there will be no comeuppance as such for in that completeness of the understanding of the ebb and the flow of the maturation of the soul, there is nothing that could ever be done that could not be done in another way and another time without putting any pressure on the soul whatsoever for the Universe, the God force is eternally grateful, gentle and loving.

So we put it in a relationship context but with the same token you may have this with a mother, with a father, you may have this with money, with what you look at and the connection and the experiences with money and the belief that you have never had enough money and you never will have enough money, so you will reverberate and you will meet that energy of every experience that you have ever had with money, every relationship to money that you have ever had, every belief that has ever governed your way of living. If you have had many lives filled with money and you have come back and you have been a beggar then you will understand the contrast and the paradox of that contrast and then you may come back in and say I will come in as the beggar again and I will make myself a millionaire in this one and then off you go, done.

So the law of karma will set up the energy but it is not coming from any other source but you and it is all negotiated before you give birth to yourself again and it is all by your grand design. This is why we say when we teach that unity of consciousness that there is nothing that has ever been lost and there is nothing that cannot ever be experienced, every possibility always exists in any moment of any time, that is the essence of karma and how fast you move through one situation, you will still never ever finish the job, it cannot be any other way.

Now we say to you what the heck is a contract and an agreement and we say that it is merely a way of voicing, it is the new language of voicing, action and reaction, intention and experience for there is not an agreement that is signed on the dotted line, typed up and organised but there is an understanding of the essence of the experience. The individual will then be accountable for its response mechanism in the moment of the experience, so we have response and we have experience and we have action and we have reaction, karma.

So we will dispel this myth of a judgement day for it can never be and if you truly think that the Christ source is coming back to judge and to decide who is a good person and who is not a good person, you will understand in the light of what we have just told you what utter nonsense that truly is and it is not that we do not respect the religions of your world but we say that it is time for them to take another look at the essence and source of Christ for the essence and source of Christ was never to make a judgement on anything for the essence and soul of Christ was karma in perfection if you would truly understand its source. It came into male form because that is what would be respected at that time on your earth, he had to mirror what you expected in that energy source, male domination, patriarchal energy but he could have chosen to come in as a woman had you lived in the pagan goddess energy of that time when he was scripted to come in and teach you and here is the truth of your Christ energy.

He was here to teach you about karma, he was here to teach you about responsibility and action and reaction, personal responsibility for all deeds done on earth but not to chastise you but to help you to understand that you need to lighten up, that you need to enjoy the experience of living and stop making expectations on yourself that cannot be met. When you give up this, then you will truly enjoy your life, it is a shame that most of you pass from this life into the next life without truly looking over your shoulder and enjoying the life that you have been living, understanding that you cannot make a mistake, that you are exactly where you are meant to be and that in any moment the law of cause and effect state to you simply that you have the responsibility to make the choice in that moment and it is in that choice and in that action that you will then set up the understanding of what it is that you are being sent back onto the earth to experience, it is just that simple.

If you are a part of that God source and you will return to

God source then you will review this, tweak it we would say in your language today, so to us being a poet is purely metaphysical, you are reading the poetry of all of your lives and any one of you can tap into that history, all you have to do is learn to be silent, learn to go within and allow your soul to speak to you. Now your intuitive guidance system will then be like a red flag and it will say "perhaps you could make a wiser choice, that doesn't feel right" and we say follow that because it is telling you that you can make a wiser choice in that moment.

Now imagine if we could understand that between nations, imagine if we could understand that as we divide and conquer we can mirror to each other the two sides are actually in agreement that the collective consciousness of the Germanic and the collective consciousness of the Brittany have decided to get together and that one will be the perpetrator and one will be the victim and they will learn about nations and boundaries, strength, war and defeat, death and living and that on the global mass there will be a lesson that will be learned but it will be reverberated over and over and over again until the two sides look at each other and say "for God's sake will you just stop that, perhaps there is a better way, why don't we talk to each other".

We would say to you karmically on all the different pockets of the earth that this is manifesting over and over and over again and you are seeing it but you are not seeing it. West, East, Muslim, Christian, whichever label you want to choose, Germanic, Brittany, it is being replayed over and over and over again and still you do not understand that this is a karmic connection that has come down through the winds of time. It is both by agreement at this time in history that these people have these beliefs etc. and you all come back from Source with this global Gallipoli, you have individual karma, you have global karma and the individual makes up the global karma and so the popular idea becomes the idea that leads the nation, then you will elect the person who will fulfil your desires. If you can truly understand that, you get someone to throw a shoe *(the President George Bush incident where a journalist in Iraq took off his shoes and threw them at him while he gave an interview)* as we were laughing at before and eventually you say "shall we just talk" but you are not at this point because you do not understand the fundamentals of this law of karma.

Now we say to you that you move from this place of understanding, you call this transition, you call this moving from physical awareness into spiritual enlightenment and you understand so you put a little note in the pigeon hole and you say "things to do, got to go back to the earth, got to meet with that person who just drove me nuts and they betrayed me and I must re-look at that, so I have now decided that at age such and such this person will come in and put that thought out". So the web and the weaving starts negotiating and then the tapestry is building but you have to understand that if you perceive that person and that person is still on the earth plane, then that connection, that karmic connection cannot be negotiated and completed until the other person meets you on the spiritual level and leaves the lower life and comes into the higher life, then they also have to go through their review and their process and then they decide exactly what they feel they need for their soul. They may not feel they want to meet you again at that time and that is fair too, so that will sit there but it could come back and it will be renegotiated and when the two agree it will be replayed out again, there is no question of it but there is no hurry, there is no need to, there is nothing to say that it all has to be done in this instant or in this next life.

So you as an individual spark of the Divine pool, that sea, the sea of enlightenment, moves into the next phase and the next phase is almost like a holding cell, it is truly a world between worlds. Now you have called it the great halls, I believe you have called it the akashic records but again we would say to you what are the akashic records but a memory and an experience of an act that has come from the earth and you now think that you can go to a library and pull a book, a book of knowledge? This is very comical to us on this side as teachers for it is not a library, there are no great halls, although you may construct that if that is what you need but that is not it and you have access to this infinite pool of great wisdom and we would say more than anything that your akashic records are found in your electromagnetic frequency when you are on the earth as much as what it is when you are in the spirit – what do you think your energy field is?

Would you be the same in essence as the energy as you emit when you are in spirit? It is an interesting question and we will leave you that one to ponder because we feel that as you ponder it you will start to get a true sense of who you are when you are in spirit and what spirit is. So you move on to an infinite place of wisdom, infinite wisdom is a vibration, it is an energy source no different from the energy source that you were just experiencing, when you were experiencing your karma. We would say to you that it is merely a collective pool of memory, remember we have already told you that there is nothing that can ever be lost, everything that has ever been thought, everything that has ever been experienced and everything that has ever been dreamt or conceived of, now that is truly the akashic records if you wanted to call it that, we call it the unity of consciousness, the unified field, the enlightenment tapestry and you have access to that now and you have certainly a higher level of access when you are not in a cumbersome body and in weight but you can still access that energy because that is the very energy and essence that you are pulling through your source, through your physicality to breathe life and movement into the body.

All of your karmic history is compounded, ruminating, reverberating, whatever you want to call it around this field, now you have called it the auric field and you have labelled it with colours but this is not really an auric field, it is a history, it is a map and it is vibration and electromagnetics, it is the Divine matrix and it is the same as that consciousness and the akashic records that you have been discussing on your earth plane – there is no separation from the two. The one that comes through you and the one that lives around you is denser in nature and that is why you can perceive it as colour but the essence and the source is exactly the same, it is spirit, there is no name for this for it is truly feeling and can you name and touch a feeling? You cannot name, you cannot touch feeling yet you know that you can experience feeling, the feeling is the karma, the feeling is the energetic source that moves you through experience – so is karma feeling? On some level, yes it is. The akashic records – we could call that thought.

You are accustomed to believing that your thoughts live in your head but we are here to tell you that your thoughts are more outside of your head than in your head, you are merely tapping in to the external thought patterns that are drawn through. So there is no distinguishing between karma, feeling and thought for if you are to take an action, you would have to have a thought about that action, then you would have to feel how that action would feel, putting it like this – if you were to go up to somebody and you were told in your own head by your own thoughts, go up and slap that person and you would instantly check out how that would feel – I don't like that person so that might feel good, bang and you take the action, there's the karma. You may also say I don't think that would be a good thing for me to do because that doesn't feel right, you have said that language all of your life, it doesn't feel right and that is karma because whether or not you still go up and slap that person, that feeling told you in your akashic record, in your pattern, that the intention of that action was not how you would like to behave or should be behaving – now that is the essence of karma.

Friends, when you move into the higher realm, spirit, it will be that little voice that says in your heart I don't think that I should do that, that will be the karmic tie that will bring you back in action and reaction with that source that you slapped, the slapping is neither here nor there but it is your knowing, now that is the akashic record, that is the energy of karma. This is what we would like to help the earth, those still living within the body to understand and that feeds into the belief pattern of consciousness and creating because if you truly understand the intention behind the action and the intention and the feeling that that is promoting, then you can tap in to many layers of that karmic tie. Think of it like coming from your heart, a ten layer cake all connecting in a 3D holographic image from your heart and in that moment you have the lower action of not even recognising karmically that if you invade that person and slap them then something would be seriously amiss in your own soul and so it does not register consciously and it becomes an involuntary action, a low energy or think of another source of that little voice over many eons of lifetimes you have gone through one layer of cake, two layers of cake, three layers of cake, four layers of cake, five layers of cake and your getting up to six layers of cake and that same action, that same experience comes to meet you on the sixth level of the cake.

Time and time again you have just reacted and responded in the way that you have always done and you have missed those signals and then all of a sudden, bang, you hear that voice and it says "maybe I shouldn't do that" but you still do it and when you get back to Source you say – well I got up to level six and I actually got that, now I will come back and I will do it again. When we get to layer seven we will be hearing that same voice, it will be a different situation but in essence it will be the same situation and you will relive it again and bang you will do it right and when your soul gets back it will throw a party and it will be very happy and it will move on and that lesson has been completed but there has been no one judging you and this is the true essence of karma, this is it, there is no other.

You will never get up to layer ten because when layer ten comes you will get the layers of ten and the next layers of ten because the unified field and the expansiveness of the Universe suggest that there is never anything that can ever be completed or done because you are as expansive as the Universe and the Universe is unlimited and untapped potential. So your akashic records can never be attained to the highest level and anybody who is trying to tell you that they have done that, well they are just speaking through ego because you can never get to the highest level of consciousness and you can never get the job done, it is not possible.

Your expectations of perfection set you up again and again to fail, so we are saying to you, listen to the feeling because the feeling and the thought that comes with the feeling is the karmic link in all situations, it cannot be anything other than that. Make your choice in that moment and do not feel that you have failed for at any moment in every situation at any time you can re-look at that and make a different choice and start from that point and you can continue that. Do you understand the level of power that will actually bring to you, the individual expressions of the consciousness because you know that you can never be wrong, you can never fail, you are merely in transition from that experience into the next experience and the maturation of that experience so you will start to lighten up, you will start to experience what is a joy and if you fall down it is only that you feel humiliated and embarrassed and that is only your ego.

Your ego will dictate that you will not even try to make that choice and now that we have spoken of this, we will ask you if there are any questions that you would like to ask about this or if there is anything that you do not understand.

(See Questions and Answers)

We thank you for your time and the honour that you pay us by feeling that these words that are being brought through to you with love, always understand that all of this information that is being shared you already have this in your akashic records for there is nothing that we can tell you that you do not already know and with that we will leave you with much love and many blessings, farewell friends.

15 - LILONG LI – DECEMBER 30, 2008

*...how did you come from one state of existence and
the birth and the physical form, how did that occur?*

 Greetings friends, we have spoken before and touched on the yugas from the Buddhist philosophy for this is the vehicle, that particular modality of information was recorded, however these yugas are known to all of the Germanic tribes and all of the tribes people, they have their own way of describing it.

You have met me before and I will say it is indeed a pleasure to be back with you today. I, myself lived in the Tibetan monastery so you will know me and as you know I was a seer and although I could see your, we shall call it what the other fellow called it, your personal akashic map. I could see your karmic imprint, I could look and tell you of that which had passed and that which was to come but today I wish to take you further, I wish to take you from personal and I wish to take you from age to age, from what you have been told is the descent from on high to placing your feet within the earth.

Of course, before you became physical you were in your spiritual form, we would say that you would perhaps understand it as between states, you were not fully of the ocean, of the waters of the great Father, Mother God, but you were not carbon, you did not have a footprint for you cannot leave one sphere of existence and fully emerge in the other form as physical matter. Even the transition from birth into the earth for all species, there is a time of impregnation, of changing as the caterpillar changes in the cocoon and your Golden Age upon your earth was this cocoon, this was the time when you became earthbound, this was the time when you left the state of all-knowing, of all-being, of oneness, of ism, you had no past concerns, you had no past ties, you were formless and yet you were fully formed. You had everything contained within the print and yet you had no physical expression – how did you come from one state of existence and the birth and the physical form, how did that occur?

We believe that as you have walked the earth you have had many great debates about this, there are those who say "God in his infinite wisdom created man from the very earth that was beneath his feet when he was in creation" but we say to you for as powerful as the Divine Matrix of all existence truly did create you, it was not just "and the word is God and God created the earth". No, it was far more than this – we have heard it said on your earth plane that you have accessed a level of intelligence, this intelligence has been named and we like the name, it is intelligent design and this intelligent design is that imagery of the expression of all of the energy waves of light that have ever been created within the earth frame.

Did you understand that there was an element of gravity; there are gravitons that literally pull the atomic structure and hold each cell and atom as a building block. Think of yourself when you see an explosion of light, now think of it being the reverse; it was an implosion of forces. The Big Bang theory that you have all been subjected to in the evolutionary scheme of things and there is a reason that we are bringing this to you because we have spoken before, the others who have come to tell you that creation, intelligent design, evolution are all one and the same and every aspect of it had to become and be. Within this implosion of the forces, the subatomic forces, if you have one atom, one neutron within that atom, the strong nucleus and the weak nucleus and the constant movement of the energy that is contained within that nucleus, that is the force that pulls the atoms together and when there is one, that one is the whole of you, you see God had only to create the atom and it was created by light, the synthesis of the light.

When you say that you are light beings, you are light, it was the slowing down of the frequencies and the waves and the patterns of the light that created the first cells. There are so many myths that you came from beings from other dimensions and planets and we will say to you that over time there are those who have come to study and to get to know you, they have walked among you but they have taken your form, they have always taken your form, you have known them as magicians, you have known them as the great geniuses of your planet but we divert away from the central piece of what we wish to help unravel about you.

Every possibility of the human mass is accessible in the one atomic structure and it is through the massing and the multiplying and the merging and the forces of the light, the gravity, the structures of the air, the structures of every particle, the minerals of the earth, the water within the oceans, every particle that was ever placed into the mix of living is contained within that one atom and that atom is humanity and this was Adam, you gave it a name and you called it Adam. What do cells do but divide, grow and from the one cell you colonised and became specialists in the fields so when some of the atoms took on specific roles and you became a mass, a mass of digestion, a mass of electronic impulses in the brain, the nervous system, you had to create a pathway for the life and the light and the energy of that nucleus to be transmitted, divided, each area of the mass specialising, each area working in the creative production, now this is where we bring in evolution in its most majestic form for if you create one cell from the whole of all of the cells and it is a mirror image, we have to have adaptability and sustainability or you would be just walking around as one big brain or one big circulatory or one big digestive tract.

Adaptability and specialisation gave homosapien the edge to create consciousness and it started within the mass and we say to you that from the world between the worlds where truly you are conscious of the earth and conscious of the non-physical aspect of you. When the two are hybrid and they meet then life is created within the form, this is what was known when the Golden Age on earth was truly known to you for as your bodies refined and you were in form while your bodies were evolving, they may not have been evolving in the muscular system for when you finally took form and merged with that atomic structure, you were complete. All that you did from that point on was to evolve, the digestive tract became more efficient, and the foods you could eat became wider and suited the diet that was available in each area that you inhabited.

If you think that this was only happening on a human level, then our talk of last time when Bartholomew came to greet you, when before that you spoke and worked with the plants and the animals from the native American Kukuwana, when this energy came to teach you their sacred skills of the plants, all of this was happening and here is where you must understand true unity to conscious, instantaneous unity for as much as this was happening to human form, it was mirrored in the animal structures and the vegetation structures and the mineral structures, it was truly evolving.

Now, we will say to you that the elements of the earth are on a slower vibration and this is where time becomes relative for everything was created in instantaneous time, no separation and yet the elemental, mineral part of your world has been in existence for many, many eons before man appeared – how can this be? The next level of the plants creating the oxygen, although it was all in creation, it has also appeared to you to have been around for eons before the human showed up and yet you were all in creation at once and the same with your animals. So you get a sense of, when we say the cell of the human body, you were in creation between the worlds for as long as the earth was in creation in a physical form where there was earth and water and atmosphere, you were already created but the physical form could not take individuation yet for the cellular structure had not been in creation, you needed the biology and yet you were as the ocean is, in existence and covering all of creation.

The speed of light is the synthesis that created the modality of the cells and those cells had to produce through the evolving stages of maturation – do you think that as a consciousness you were hanging around waiting for that birth for everything you see in creation today is a result of this time between the worlds. Everything that you could have experienced on the earth is all existing as we explained last time in the layers of the cake, as the possibilities and as quickly as you can create you can un-create and then that existence will no longer be and this is what will happen to the human being if they continue.

Now we say to you what of this Golden Age? The moment that we will say the Golden Age was when consciousness met mass and the two became one for a time. You will understand that you lived a very long life, you will understand that in those very first evolving stages of the union of the two you were not subject totally to the laws of gravity and totally to the laws of unity. You lived in a state between the worlds where you remembered everything in creation because you were a part of that creation and yet you were like newborn babes, learning how to walk, how to breathe, how to create and live, you did not speak a language for the voice box was still in creation, the dialect, the cell vibration was not necessary because you were still a thought pattern, you were still connected and you are still connected by the thought but now you no longer hear the thought because your ears are more attuned to sound vibration of a lower frequency and this is what happened on the descent from energy, Source, into matter.

We will say that as you descended from the heavens and your feet touched the earth, it was like a blanket of separateness that was descended upon you and the anxiety created was like that of a child being wrenched from its mother and vulnerability was born on the earth, fear was born into man. Separation was created for in that state there was no separation and you knew all and when the time was right you became human and a unified field of agreement of releasing the connection to Divinity and plugging yourself into a physical system of power and as everything was created at once, your futures, the future lives, the future meetings and the future creations was created at that time but you became separate from that knowledge so that your ultimate goal and this is something that we must urge you to understand, that there is not one person having a physical life at any random time but that all of life is having a physical experience in every life.

So the future you is in creation and is experiencing who you are in that life as real as you today. The Golden Age was the time when you knew this truth, when you still had union and the creative, karmic links were being formed, when your own history was being created. So when you met with another soul you saw them as self, now we take a left turn for in this hybrid state you would not move forward for before action you understood the consequences and so the universal forces drew in from and this is where the gods in heaven were created as the myth of the human experience.

The unified field will tell you that if this was happening in one place in the solar system, there is always a centre point that is the mirror of that creation and the beings that were created in that experience could be drawn through that centre point and brought to your time in reflection at any point of the evolutionary pathway and so from the higher level of awareness of this pool, this reflection, this paradoxical planetary system, you were allowed access for they had matured in that time that was mirrored to you and appeared as people from the sky. They birthed in a different genetics to be sure, they birthed in a different understanding and when the job was done and the river of forgetfulness, we will call it, was sealed - now you moved out of that golden Yuga.

It was three hundred years to the centre point of the shift and three hundred years into the new age which became the age that you have known as the Silver Age. Silver, for in its own experience the very fabric of that age became harder, the light within you became dimmer, the separation, the anxieties, the forgetfulness, the fog became thicker and as you viewed each other you became separate. Your ears were recalibrated and retuned, your voice was now heard on a lower octave and dialogue and language became the norm. In your hearts you remembered the time of separation and of those god-like energies who came to close that door and you mourned that loss and you created ritual to reconnect, folklore, artwork to remember the time of union with the great ones but you were separate and yet you have never been separate or separated.

The lives that you led in this age became the focus of your karmic ties into the future, competition, making your tribe survive, survival, sanctifying life and taking life became the order of your awareness for you could no longer ponder the heavens above for you had to survive the earth below. This is where you started to write the tale of your future experience and karmic links with each other, the Age of the silver Moon, the Sun in Heaven, sanity, godlike, the Moon, silver, dark, descending, lonely, your carnal attributes, your humanistic shortcomings became known to you and insecurity and fear were your guiding lights.

As you moved from the Age of Silver into the depth of the Bronze civilised people gathering, tool carving, you were now fully in the separateness of the self, you created the tribe fully, you created borders, humankind etched out and began to grow, learning that separation from each other created weakness, you were driven to create strength in numbers and all of that Age was creating your structure of society and still there was that faint light in the sky that called you home for even in the depth of the darkness of war and death and famine in fear and separation, there were always the ties to the heavens above, to the force of God but now you did it through the modality of separation, whereas in the Golden it was in the Light of union and all. This is where time truly slowed down, this is where you became aware of time and all of this time you were creating the pool of the global consciousness of all of the earth, like a spiral above the earth, all of the consciousness amassing, guiding the individual consciousness forward – what was the order to be, death?

So you became focused and your bodies became all important, the senses became the whole of your reality, your life became your body and now true separation. The paradox is you were always and are always striving to be united into unity, this is the madness of the whole system and now you walk through a door of Iron, the iron horse, power, male predominance, blackness and separation for you must walk through the ego in the Age of Iron. All of the Ages preceding this Age was building the global ego and the individual manifestation of that ego, this is the Age of ego, this is the Age where male power overtook nurturing which is your natural state of being but was seen as being weak and so to be weak meant death, so power became the force to drive you forward.

What do you find at the end of that Age – enlightenment, from the depth of ego, why would there be the mass destruction of humanity, think of it as a purging of one's soul and you will do it because you wish to be part of that stripping and baring naked before the majestic light of yourself in the remembrance of who you are. The three hundred years is that bit by bit stripping of the ego, the nurturing part of your nature is coming back, you do it through the green movements, through the inequity that you see through your fear of death and destruction, your soul is awakened and realigned to the Age of Enlightenment – separateness no longer exists and you see each other as brother and sister. Now we say to you that the river of forgetfulness re-emerges and the paradoxical Universe is in alignment once again.

Through each Age there is a planetary and a universal alignment and when the peoples of the earth are mature enough to meet that, this is when the two points merge. The phenomenal part of this emergence is when the two points meet at a union point, the two galaxies meet at that point with the same enlightenment and the fork in the road joins. We have spoken of the two lines, comfort, greed and profit, ego, the Iron Age and service, selflessness, unconditional servitude and love, the two points meet in harmony and you move in, not to the Golden Age for you have done that, it would serve you no purpose to go back to that unified pool of existence and is-ness, it will be the Age of Peace and peace vibrates to the colour vibration and speed of the blue rays. In that peace, when the two universes meet and you create the future, for we will also allude to the fact that as much as the two merge at that point, your very definition of time and experience and action, that is the essence of that peace, will completely change – as your Mayans called it the Age of No Time.

You will be introduced to a time of instantaneous ism and if you were to think you shall be able to access that thought in creation, the two worlds are bridged – do you understand the level of power that you harness through your physical manifestation called your body? We hold very little hope from our point in the universal conscious pool that you will make this transition for your war and your ego and your power are still fully engaged and to harness that power as the nuclear bombs that were sent to rain death on your earth, at this point in your conscious evolution, we see you repeating that process from where you are today where you would contain that power and use it against your brother, nation over nation but we celebrate for as the layers of the cake, all possibilities are always in manifestation. From your Age of Iron, power and ego as you emerge, all possibilities from this point and every other point on the continuum line are available for a conscious renegotiation of the outcome and where your experience would shift in its nature.

Now again we take you to the pool and the energy swirling above the earth, the polarisation of the North and the South and we say that that consciousness is the point where the two lines meet and whatever the consciousness of the masses are experiencing, that is the point in creation that you manifest and your experience can change in an instant, no time and all that has been created to this point shall be the history of the fogs of time, the mists, the memories.

Man is a force of nature, there is never a life that has been lived that has not served that force of nature, every experience that has been conscious and played out upon the earth is a representation of the single atomic structure at the beginning of creation and you are creating a world outside of your own biological structure mapped on that structure – that is the akashic record and the imprint of your life. You cannot outrun it, you cannot negotiate it, you can experience it, it will mature within you and as that matures within you through lifetime after lifetime of experience, your physical building blocks to emote the expression through becomes a higher vibrational frequency match to that, the individual force that was created within the atomic structure, the nucleus, when you view the nuclear explosion, that is the source of your life where the two aspects of the self mirror and meet. As you create life, you go through every stage of that evolution within the first 12 weeks of gestation, from bacteria to amphibian to human, all the stages are manifest in the division of the cells, all of the stages of the evolution of the species are contained within the separation of the cells which is how you are born and created today.

There is no other form, there is no other way, and there is the human being which is the pinnacle of creation. As you move into the next stage of your human evolution, if you do not align the two lines of creation, the parallel universal forces, it does not matter for within that bracket of that Yuga being created you will take the path of attaining and creating worms, as you call them, through the fabric of time and when you have broken that code which we might add is in the cell membrane, this is where you will find the technology to manage time, slip through the continuum, you will learn to vibrate more light in each cell, you will take the form of light beings, you will communicate again through the mental field and eventually you travel and pass objects through the dimensional pull and the worms created the blackness of time. The blackness of time and space feel heavier than the other that you may see and yet they are the pathway into the new paradigm and as you do this, again 2600 years from the shift of the Age, you will have the opportunity of alignment of the two polarisations and at this point, through the blue rays of peace and harmony, through the holographic understanding of the whole of creation, you will map the first Yuga, the Golden Age where energy became unified into life on earth and the wonder of who you are will be remembered and union will be attained, not to an outside force but you will return whole and complete.

As you return whole and complete, separation will no longer be real for you, the shift into the unified field of all is complete and the consciousness of the earth, and to give you an image, the swirling energy on the polarisation of the earth which is the consciousness of its inhabitants, like a cell exploding the light, will be seen into infinity and from every frequency of life within the galaxy and the known Universe. Your earth shall become that as what happened within the splitting of the atom and the two earths shall merge as one field and all of the Universe in its infinitesimal and infinite structures will be able to vibrationally match your peoples of the earth.

We will close now and it has been our pleasure to bring this knowledge and as it is of such an important nature of understanding we would say to you that everything that we bring has been perfectly scripted from the beginning where we came in on a level of understanding the self, the individual self, always bringing in the one truth, there is no separation, there is never separation and that the one truth in everything that we have ever taught has been that you are, you are, you can never be anything other than the unified field of consciousness contained within the ninth centre of your reality.

God bless.

16 - Lilong Li – January 4, 2009

*…you say "I have truly not created that which I
wanted to create, how is it that I cannot create
what my greatest desires are"…*

 Greetings friends – allow me to introduce myself to you today, my name is Lilong Li and I have been working through this instrument for a number of months and have been working with her the whole time that she has been doing her demonstrations. As a trance medium this is what she does when she does trance and when she does demonstrations, she brings the loved ones through and allows them to speak for themselves and to make that connection with you which is what we would like to speak about today. It is about you remembering who you are, it is about you remembering that you are spirit and that you are in this physical form for a very short time and we would like to spend this time with you and we are very grateful for the opportunity to be here with you today.

We would like to talk to you about what powerful manifestors you are and that if you would truly understand that you are more than just this physical body and trying to work through eliminating and re-connecting with your higher self then you would understand that you were totally the creators of your reality.

The creator of your reality, it is very, very popular these days and yet we hear from you repeatedly, you create your own reality, do your affirmation work and that you put out those thoughts of consciously co-creating and then you turn to yourselves and you say "I have truly not created that which I wanted to create, how is it that I cannot create what my greatest desires are" and those greatest desires will take you to the next level of your development if you would let them but before you can truly tune in to the belief pattern that you are the conscious co-creators of your reality, you will sabotage the journey because you will be forever attuning yourself to the belief pattern that you cannot totally create what it is that you wish to experience.

You have been taught over and over again that you must be of service and be giving of self and to be giving of all those around you and yet you live in a world full of selfishness and full of taking – how can this paradox be bridged, how can you take this on board, how can you truly create health when you are faced with illness? We would like to introduce to you at this time the concept of vertical time, the consciousness and the awareness of instantaneous time. You are accustomed to looking at your beliefs through the third dimensional space and the fourth dimension where vertical time exists, well this is time and where we live is the space of no time.

We would say to you that there has never been anything that has ever been thought, there has never been anything that has ever been created, there has never been anything that you have experienced that is not consciously available to you all in any given moment and this is the concept of that vertical time. You have heard of the Law of Attraction – do you understand the idea of the Law of Attraction, do you understand that if you put that thought out, it must first permeate the mental body. You have four bodies, you have a physical body with which you conduct your day to day lives, you have an emotional body and you have the mental field, the mental body but you also have a spiritual body. This spiritual body is where you will find that you will connect with that Law of Attraction for you cannot bring to you any thoughts that you have not already conceived and created, it is not possible.

So when you are born into the earth, you are born complete, when you are born into the earth, you are born all knowing, you know that there is no time, you know that there is only ism, instantaneous, it is used through the awareness of the physical self and separate from Source that creates the mental field of resistance. When you give this up, when you truly become aware of self, self as you were before you became separate, before you became that selfish person and in your earth you say that selfishness is a bad thing but we say to you this is exactly why you have come onto the earth. So if you stay in the Great Spirit realm then you will never know what it is to receive for the self alone, you will never know what it is to want because in that fourth dimensional no time you are complete connection to the whole of the eternal Source.

You are like a ripple in the waters of time, when you place a pebble on those waters, the ripple moves through the body of the water and that is what happens with the Law of Attraction, this is what you do with every thought in your being, this is who you are, you have become accustomed to believing that your thoughts live within the mind and we say to you that with every thought you express through this mental field you are creating the ripple and it is the ripple that creates the vertical time. In this vertical time, you could liken it to every possibility available to you in that instantaneous moment, every possibility that you have ever experienced or ever wanted to experience, from the lowest of the low to the highest of the high, the ripple that is emanating from the thought is what is sent into the heart. The emotional body emanating from the thought is what is sent into the heart, the emotional body then sends out the wave. If you have always thought limitation, then that is exactly what that ripple in the vertical time will connect and draw back to confirm the experience, if on the other hand you were to catch yourself in that moment, this is what it is to become a conscious being – do you understand that when you become a conscious being that you are saying "I have lived the whole of my earth life in the state of sleep, I have not been consciously aware of what it is that I have been manifesting and creating".

So you have a thought and you drop it to the heart and you send this heart mind out in the wave and vertical time in the fourth dimension, no time, is holding every possibility and then you experience that magnetic attraction and it comes back and it either confirms the experience and you say "I knew that would happen to me, it always happens that way, how could I have possibly expected that it could be anything different" but we would say to you that when you become conscious, this is when you catch yourself in that modality and you say "no, I can make a different choice today, just because it has always been, it does not mean that it shall always be, so I will set a new program".

This is where your affirmation work will truly start to become the manifestor for as you finish the program of limitation and what I cannot achieve, my beliefs and you turn that around and you say "I can create and I am abundant and the wealth of the Universe is all around me, it is up to me to see that wealth, it is up to me to bring that to me and I am the conscious co-creator of my reality". In that instant the ripple that is being placed the time space continuum is changed and the vibration is lifted, the vibration then comes back to you and the signal and the positive fruits of those actions are now experienced in your life.

You have been doing this all of your life, you are so good at doing this but you do it so unconsciously that you send that ripple out we would almost liken it to a program, or pre-programmed conditions. You wish to experience money, you wish to experience health, and we would say to you that to experience health that you must truly see yourself in that instantaneous place of being healthy. If you believe that you are healthy, if you believe that you are fully aligned, fully abundant and you live that every day of your life, then that is what has to meet you. If you get up in the morning and say "good God, it is morning, how will I get through the day, I am so unwell", everything from that point will meet you on that vibration.

The key to this is to understand that your physical form is 1% of who you truly are, the mass of you remains in the higher vibration as your true source, essence, you are that source in physical manifestation and when you start to see this, you then start to break down what all of the Masters who have come to this earth to teach you – do not be personally invested in your lives, step back from the experience, look with the eyes of the soul, look at the people who have been magnetically attracted into your life, know that they could not enter your orbit of being unless you expressed a connection and a desire to meet with them on the physical realm at that time, space continuum – this is how it has always been, you are truly that powerful when you understand not to take your life so personally.

Now here is a thought that we would like to share with you for if you are that source, every soul, every person, any energy vibration in this room and in your life is also that source and is that Source that we have called God, then the person who has come to try you, the person who you cannot connect with, then they are mirroring the experience that you have set up yourself. This is hard to grasp at first but this is a divine law of the Universe so when you look at those people, a great Master came onto the earth and he asked the Lord "who shall I say has sent me" and that was Moses and the voice that met with him said to him "I am that, I am", I am you, they are you, every person and every animal, every plant and every atom is that God Source and to truly understand this, you will then understand that if you lash out at that person in anger, you are lashing out at self for they are you.

So I ask you to take a look at the people who are in your life, to separate the emotional response – are you reactive in every moment of your being, do you react to all of the world in front of your eyes or are you the master of your own being, can you truly in that moment, when that person you are perceiving to do the wrong thing by you, see them as self and walk through the door of compassion. If you understood Christ's message on earth, this was at the heart of the teaching, this was why that Master came to the earth for he wished you to understand that if you see the God in him, then you must see the God in yourself – now the God force, that is who you are, you can never be separate but you must walk through the door of separation for in walking through the door of separation, then you truly understand the urgency to be vibrationally pulled back to Source.

So the question remains – for what purpose was I born and as this thought leaps out of your mind, it engages your heart and you look at the world in front of your eyes and you say "there must be more to life than just this" and then the journey of going into self begins for you may get information from the books but every thought, every moment experienced on the earth is always in creation. If you want to know for what purpose you are living in this moment, then there is only one source that can come to teach you this and it is self.

All of the other people and circumstances come to give weight and experience to the journey and then the journey draws to a close and because you are living separation, you fear what you believe is the unknown and yet from where we are standing you are never separate and there is no unknown. We would say that you spend your life in distraction; we would say that you lose your power source on the earth, the God force as you get caught up in life's trivialities and you lose the intensity of the journey of understanding who you are. This is perhaps a different way to view the world for you are trained well by your parents and your social construct, you have to experience the separation but as that day comes when you are being called home, you are merely redefining and a part of you is dying and it is that part of you that has been living the separation, the lower part of the consciousness.

This is what spiritualism has been teaching you all along, you will transcend death, you will move into fourth dimensional time, you will become source, you will then be born back into the earth to bring that golden nugget of grace to all of the people with whom you will meet and it is agreed upon before you enter your earthly domain. The Law of Attraction is your natural state of being, do not separate yourself from that, when your life gets crazy, when you mourn or are feeling alone, when the dark night of the soul comes to greet you, understand as John of the Cross and the great teachers of the past were coming to share with you, this is part of the soul's maturation, this is how you transcend the separation and the physical limitations, all of the false beliefs that you have been blinded by will have to leave, they will die. So it will feel like a grief no different from when you witness a friend or a loved one die but we guarantee you as the illusions and the false beliefs slowly ebb away and you vibrationally ascend to that higher order which is living in that vertical time, the higher perception that has always been available to you but you have never been able to magnetically draw it in to your essence and your being for you have not been a vibrational match.

When you discard the weight, the blindness, the pain and you ascend to the higher order and the new truth, now you are the deliberate creator, now you transcend and you move in to that new place, that new life and you look over your shoulder as the months and years of time and space and you say "that was so hard and yet I love where I am for it has taken me on a journey I never thought possible and I am happier than I have ever been and maybe, just maybe, if I can do this once I can do it again and again.

Please always know that you are, you have never been anything other, you are divine in nature, you are gods on earth but that does not mean that you are superior for you are all gods on earth, the lowest of the low contains the God essence, awaken the heart to compassion for in compassion you will always find peace and forgiveness and that forgiveness shall set you free and heal your entire life

God bless and thank you for allowing me to share with you.

17 - BAAL SHEM TOV – JANUARY 8, 2009

...What you can create is truly about recognising the level of power that you are within and not the power that is on the external vibration...

 Welcome, it is always our pleasure to be of assistance to you as you work to open your knowledge pool, the individual spark that will ultimately reunite you with your true source. We brought a thought with us today of birth, death and creation and the understanding of creating your own reality, of creating financial independence and security, of creating health, of living abundance, of finding joy in the experience of your life, all too often you get so caught up in what is going on in front of your eyes in what you call reality and we call the dream, all of your focus, all of the attention, all of the separation, the fears and the anxieties that hold you back while you push forward, limitation and it all comes down to an awareness of who you are, not who your personality is but who you are at your core, of who you are in your essence.

What you can create is truly about recognising the level of power that you are within and not the power that is on the external vibration. All too often you are giving your power, your strength and your energy to misperception of mass consciousness.

If you are always following the tribe, if you are always ready to put yourself beneath another, if you do not feel important, if you are not the leader but choose the follower, how on earth can you become the creator of that reality? Far from being the creator of your reality, your reality is creating your experience – isn't that a different way of looking at it? Although you are still creating, for you must always create, perhaps we should have called it creation and birth, for you must always be in creation if you are to be on a life vibration of the earth.

There are many levels with which we can talk to you today on this very subject but first allow me to introduce myself for I was the creator of a new philosophy of being, there had been philosophy placed into the earth and it had been given a name of a religion, this religion had a lot of expectations placed upon it and the person who was trying to emulate that had to give so much of themselves in the process of being what they considered a good Jew. However, with all of what they could not do and all of what they had to do to follow this faith, they lost touch with their own sense of self, they were so busy following which they felt was the pathway to God and there was such an expectation placed upon them from those who they believed were higher in the scale and in the scheme of the religious order that they felt that they were subservient and beneath those who had become known as (I guess you would call it the hierarchy).

This was cumbersome, this was not an easy path to follow, there were certainly very good aspects that came into it as with all religions for in order to follow all of the different areas that you must adhere to, you had to have a strict sense of discipline, you had to have morality, you had to have a certain way of behaving in the world and you had to adhere to that behavioural expectation that was placed upon you to be a part of the group. This was fine and this is the very essence of how society is put together but when we separate from adhering to a belief pattern to the pathway to God which is always from within, it will never come from an external source, you cannot find your way to God if you are looking in the world and to the people in the world and you cannot find it in ritual, you cannot find it there for it does not live there – God lives within you, it is the memory of who you are, it is the knowing of where you come from, it is in the remembering of your spirit, it is of adjoining and aligning the source and there is nothing that can ever be given in the earth that will give to another person your sense of what God is.

This is what religion is, that is the structure and foundation of it for it teaches you through the presence of one bringing the teachings of the soul and then all of the mass try to emulate and follow and live up to that source that they see in front of their eyes, they build a philosophy in the teachings and they create right and wrong. This is the essence my friends of your religious orders and when it is done in purity and in the higher service, it can be effective on some level, however, it can never connect you with God for God can only be accessed in the knowing and the remembering and the merging of the souls. So you will emulate and ritualise and all of the time that you are reading the words, practicing the prayer, living the beliefs to the best of your ability, you are dissipating the power of your own spirit and you are structurally building false power, idolatry and religion is based upon this, it is a trade-off of your personal power into mass consciousness.

What we would like to say to you is that as you support and nurture the very essence of what is being born into that belief that you are placing your heart and soul into, fundamentally it is being governed by man and wherever there is man, remember that, they must first walk through comfort, greed and profit, they must first remember what it is to be selfish, they must first remember how they will take to build for themselves for this is the fundamental energy that drives humanity – how could it not be if just being on the earth has created separation, when you have drunk from the river of forgetfulness, when you have separated your source from the spring of eternity, it is liking putting a black veil around self. You can stand in the middle of a crowd but if all of your senses are dampened, if nobody can see your personality or image, do you exist or are you just a mass in space, physical space in the junction of time and this is what happens when you are born into the earth.

Your ego will engage and your personality will be formed by the external reality of your experience and you may go into religious orders, read the books but you will not truly take that humanistic element of selfishness out of the equation until you have left physical form. So what you find is as the institution builds and gains power, it attracts those who wish to take that power and utilise it for their own self, now they will justify this to themselves by saying that they are doing it for the good of all but the truth is simplicity itself when it says – you cannot do anything for anybody else without first running it through your own private agenda. The question to always ask the self, the ego, the personality, is what purpose does this serve to me, what will I gain out of that action and does that serve the higher good or is that in service to my own inner good?

This has been the structure of religion and once you have the many running, the structure and the power base is growing, you can add corruption and they will always target those who are the weaker, who may not have had the education, and when we say education, we do not mean arithmetic and math's, we mean the education of the spirit, the lower energy field, the newer souls who have not quite matured, we have explained karma, we have explained the layers of the cake, they are in the lower tiers of the cake, they are perfect and they are working through the levels of maturation as they need to experience this of the earth. The ones who lead, you may say perhaps have moved through to the top or middle part of the cake but they have not become self aware of who they are, they have not merged with the life spring of essence in its entirety yet and this is what I came onto the earth to share, this is what I came into the earth to branch away from, it is ironic to me as I sit and I understand that they did exactly to what I came to teach as they have always done to the other religious factions of Judaism, Christianity, the Muslim philosophy, the Hindu philosophy.

All of this seems to be the natural progression for wherever man lays their hands on a simple truth of the Universe; they will corrupt it with selfishness and greed. There have been the few on the earth who have come to lead the way out of the darkness, I believe it was called dharma ash kina but it has never been truly realised within the earth, now this is what will bring peace and that new age of evolution into the earth. When all of this is recognised as being an external power source that dissipates your power of source, this is truly your New Age but it is the oldest and the most reverent energy that you have ever met – do you understand that for as long as you command your spirit, your power source into any external belief pattern, you are giving your spirit over to a mass and they will use your power to create what they wish to create on the earth and that creation is about power and is about selfishness.

So we say to you that to truly ascend to the next level of spirituality you cannot look at the institutions that you have already created for they are at fault for they are governed by man and as long as they are governed by man, you can never hit that spirit, that truth, that ascension to a higher order of reality, you must first strip all of the physical falsehoods and beliefs and this leads to disillusionment and we will say that you are in the age of disillusionment. All of the power sources will have to fail you for that is how it is stripped from your energy, your energy creates form, thought into form, the emotion and the pain is the lesson learner you say and what does it teach you – to surrender and as you surrender your will then you can ascend to the next level of the journey. The surrender will not stop there for you will continue to amass more knowledge and the lessons that will come to you, the experiences (I think we like that better) will be of a finer vibrational match but you will still be placed in the surrender of your expectation, this is the maturation of the soul.

The simple truth of the progression of your spiritual power

is expectation for if you expect that another can give you the answers, you can never accumulate your own sense of urgency in the field, of your own sense of intensity of your own soul, you cannot expect to see the unexpected if all of your power is going into others. Simplicity itself is the name of this game, everything that you see with the physical eyes and sense with the physical senses, they are the enemy in your spiritual journey, the mastery of the senses is in essence the key and it is the key for ascension to the seven senses if you are impersonal about the process that is going on in front of you.

Krishna as he came into the earth was the teacher of this lesson, Jesus was the next episode in the journey, spiritual mastery is no more than mastery of you for as you master your own intuition, as you master your own reflection in the world, as you master your own actions, as you master your own intentions and as you detach from your expectations you become filled with Source and Source power. The death is the death of the false power that you have been commanding your spirit into others to run your life, to run your beliefs, you plug into the tribal power program of your earth, this is the essence of the connection in the base of the spine, this is the lesson that you learn in this centre of your being. As you pull that energy out of the mass consciousness, as you start to unravel your own mysteries and beat your own drum, as you become the power conduit for your spirit and it is not leaking like a sieve out of every part of your experience on the earth – think of a 100 watt globe.

When you are born into the earth you are that globe, bright, shining, new, vibrant, light, the emanation that you send out fills the room, imagine if that light was running and never switched off, year after year becoming duller, less energy, the wattage dropping from 100 to 90 to 80 to 70 through the decades, year after year, dimming and dimming. When you are at your highest potential of your earth life between the mid-30 year cycle to the mid-40 year cycle, you are now running dim, you have left your light on, you have given your sense of light to everything other than yourself and this is when the illnesses occur for your batteries run flat, the molecular structure cannot rebuild, the DNA has the program to create every sister cell that you need to stay healthy and run at 100 watts. The DNA comes in and it creates the copy, the machines and the keys come along to build the amino acids and the proteins and build them into the fabric of life and then the machines that come in to send those new cells, those new energy patterns, into the organs of the body to keep the 100 watts bright but this does not happen because year after year and decade after decade you have been emitting all of the energy and the light into every area of your life without check.

So you dissipate and the vibrations become lower and you get depressed, you are tired with life for life is a burden and is no longer creating joyfulness. Learning to master, learning to contain the light within the organs, within the biological framework, the light that is emitted burns bright – now we come into creation for when you create with that level of power, thought is turned into form in an instant, wealth cannot help but shower abundance upon you, health is created from within the very fabric of who you are, this is who you are trying to remember, this is knowing Source, the Divine tap, that ever present liquid gold, grace.

You know the ones who have this dynamic under control for they hold potential and potency, when they walk into the room you sense power emulating and emanating from every action and word spoken. When your Christ walked into a town, his light was of such a frequency that he could lift all of the other vibrations within that town and it was the mastery of the self that he learned in his youth. This is the essence of why you are born, why you live the karmic connection experience and the return to Source at the end of that experience with all of the perfection and imperfection of your life.

My job on earth was to help to bring about the understanding of peace and of self awareness, it has been tainted and it has been humanised but the essence of my teachings are the same today as they were hundreds of years ago, the essence of my teachings was to go within and discover the power of prayer for the individual, the recognition of the patterns of response and reaction, of becoming impersonal and yet remaining extremely personal within your life frame, within the relationships that you are creating within your life, it was the journey of excavating the own soul self.

Reaction, pro-activity, proactive in life, proactive in thought, proactive in form, reactive in nature, reactive in emotion, dynamite and a charge of intention and the misuse of will – I will say to you that there are many layers of your earth, there are many dimensions contained within the fabric of the Universe, we liken it to a loaf of bread with the slices, the earth at the centre being more dense and holding more matter, the other slices on either side containing the other realities of that earth and that universal structure. The quantum physics of those dimensions are of a different elemental makeup from the one of the earth for that is the paradigm of matter and yet the wave of light force is contained within the other layers of the loaf, each layer a different elemental fabric.

If we said that you were standing in a house of mirrors and in one mirror you looked three feet tall, in another mirror you looked six feet tall, in another mirror you looked very wide, in another mirror you looked extremely thin, in another mirror you looked upside down, all of the mirrors contain your image yet all of the images contain a different version of you as you stand in physical space, fourth dimension is the reflection of that.

In the last talk that was given we explained that you move from this other dimension, you move through the other dimension and at one point you connected with the higher evolution of your own maturation in the earth and you drew that through the mirror through the centre of your reality and you created life in physical form with the building blocks of that reality.

This is how the Universe works, this is what your God is, it is not an omnipresent being, but it is that essence of the room of mirrors, of being able to transcend those different frequencies within the mirrors. The gravitational pull of your earth keeps you engaged in the physicality of your earth and the way you perceive the cosmos but you think that gravity is so strong it holds you to the earth and yet every minute of your life on earth you defy that element, it can transcend the paradigm of your reality, third dimensional space and that is the pull through the centre of your Universe and that is the door through which you attain higher spheres of existence.

As I lived on the earth I did not fully know what I speak about today, I just knew that I could no longer be in servitude to a system of power which I perceived as corrupt, I listened to my higher vibration, intuition, I was a medium unrecognised in your language, I brought through the teachings of the higher elements of the self and of others in the collective pool of humanity and I brought that in to branch away from the disciplined structure of that mass of Judaism. I saw through the transparency and I wished to bring light and freedom to my people, I do not feel that this was done to the best of my ability at that time as I was immersed in time and space, however I did achieve the branching and the flowers and the fruit have grown since, I spoke with my heart and I gave all of myself.

Remember who you are, look at the false power in the world and then cleanse yourself of those limited beliefs that you have plugged your spirit into, become detached from the physicality of the world, of social class, of monetary power, of wealth, remove yourself from this element of greed and destruction, work with the power of your spirit in cleansing yourself in the surrender to who you are and the remembrance of your spirit. Learn to give up the expectation of the ego and surrender yourself to your spirit and you will become master of your own being, you will master your reaction and you will become proactive in the creation of your life for it is in the maintenance of that pro-activity that you become the deliberate creators of your reality.

Now we will ask if you have any questions on this or any other subject you wish to speak to us about.

(See Questions and Answers)

We thank you for your love and your patience and for your hard work at putting our words into physical form, we hope that with these words we can go beyond just the group that is before us and we can take the knowledge and the awareness and the awakening and spread it throughout humanity – now that would serve our soul's purpose and I tell you that the first layer was to create separation within the religious structures of the physical life that I lived, I now work at the same process for this is what this is all about but I do it from a higher perspective so I keep my centre of focus and direction and I do not become wrapped in a veil of separation so the teachings are pure.

We hope that we have brought some of the tools that you will need as you unravel your own inner mystery and then bring that mystery back to the world.

We bless you and we say farewell – Namaste.

QUESTIONS AND ANSWERS

PAUL — July 3 2008

Q. (Alex)   I am interested in the workings of your side of life and you say that you come from a galaxy far, far away – how did you get here?

Fair question – rockets of intention are sent out, we are not separate from you as we have already said, and we are those overlords, the overseers of your planet. When we say that we were in the earth before your time and before the earth became your earth that you know today, we were the elements of that earth – how could we not know that you wish to speak today? By the very intention of that thought that you have emitted from your brainwave, the electric impulses that you vibrate, it is like a beacon light to us – we are part of the whole, there is not a part of you that is separate from us and if you wish to speak to us, everyone of you may do exactly what this instrument is doing – there is nothing special in this interaction at all, it is absolutely extraordinarily easy for all of you to attain. By putting that intention into thought and by sending that thought, just by the very act of creating that time in space, you send that to us and like a beam of light, words are hard for us but we are working to use the words that you will recognise and to put the patterns together for you so that you can understand in your language we follow the intention.

We are the vibration and we slip through the fabric of the Universe, we are still exactly where we are all the time yet we are also present here at this moment – we are who we are and we are the breath of the Universe and yet we are also able to distinguish ourselves from this oneness into the individuality of that pattern that needs to be condensed and relayed through the instrument as the vehicle that is now present for us to use. So, we just slip through the fabric of time, you are limited by your version of time. We can be in many places at once, you can be in many places at once, there have been those who have done that on your earth plane, they have been in many places at once – it is all open and possible to you but you limit because you do not believe. There can be 30 of you in one place at one time all vibrating on a different frequency – how could we not be here with you today – you sent that intention out and we have responded as such.

Slip through the moonbeams we will call it so that you can recognise the pattern of words – slip through the moonbeams down into your etheric and into your lateral and then vibrationally attune the instrument so that we could now match your pattern to the speed with which your individual auras vibrate. You are a cellular being and there are ways that we see you that you do not see yourself, you are patterns of light and waves of possibilities and it is those waves that we follow and the particles that we amass so that we could be with you today.

Q (Alex). What is your occupation between visits?

We simply are - we have no occupation, only you have occupations. We are the overseers – please brother, understand that we are you and that you are us and everything that you and every other person are experiencing we are able and willing and a part of that by the very vibrations that you send out we meet you. We do not hang in the clouds as the medium would say, we like the vocabulary, we are in every object, we are in every person, we are in every voice, we are in every plant, we are you, we do not do anything yet we do everything. We are whole – we do not have any more words to give you on this.

We are your breath and we do love you but it is not a love that you recognise as loving one another, it is a love that is born of knowing, it is respecting and that is too limited a word, it is knowing that if you were to hurt your own child, that being who you have created life to bring forth the spirit, it would hurt and destroy you, that being is separate from you, that child, and yet it was born from you, the blueprint, the whole of the being of that person is you and yet separate from you and will grow to be separate from you, as it should be. That is who we are to you, that is what we do for you, when we say that we are the overlords, we are no different from a father/mother, we are no different from a child, so when you look at your children and you look at one another you are seeing us and we are living that experience in that moment.

Q. (Mary) President Mugabe – does people power overcome oppression?

A planetary and illumi are an earth dynamic that has been going on since time began. Unless those who live the oppressed life free themselves from within their own oppression, they do not truly believe that they can be free of their oppressor. When we say that you have the choice to create destiny and experience, unless you can truly make those changes from within your being within your consciousness, unless you can take that luminous body and the threads of that body, that tapestry, matrix, whatever you wish to call it, and unless you can change that which slips between the atoms of belief, creation, consciousness and belief in self and change, unless you can breathe those changes from within you, then how on earth can you un-connect, unshackle, change, stand tall, whatever language that you wish to use and bring down the oppressor by the very fear and belief that they are oppressing you, you are oppressed.

If you can change that belief to being empowered, and we will state that this is the prime objective of your physical life, if you look at this question you will seeing it playing out through all relationships at all times and this is part of the reason you will come into this earth plane for you will have to learn how to do this and it is only when you learn how to believe in going within the self and pull on those reserves and truly change the structure, the foundation, the blueprint, the blocks that you have put into creation, then that is when you will change the view that you see through your eyes – that is when you will change how you view the world.

This is why those in Zimbabwe are oppressed, they live oppression. When they wake in the morning, they see oppression, when they sleep at night they hover in the etheric and they feel the oppression. When they are totally in that vibration, how can they not draw to them the oppressor? The vibration, the thought, the whole of the conscious connection has been established and it is more authentic than the truth that at any moment they could turn their backs on that belief and choose a different view through the view finder when they turn back around and everything would change and in that instant that whole continent that you call Africa, that you see as an impoverished nation, would be on a par with what you call your United States but is merely that you in your countries are adding to that vibrational imprint of impoverishment and that vibration is what is the glue that keeps them locked into that, so we ask you – are your superior? You would say not and yet we ask you that if you peel back the layers, that is exactly how you see yourselves, if you go deep within the womb of your creation and your belief and your building blocks and your structures, this is what you believe. Now we challenge you – if you feel sorry for them, if you send up emotion in that moment to them that they are impoverished and that you are distressed about that, then you have just added to their oppression.

Will you give thanks that they are free and that they are whole and that they are clear and they can see clearly, then you have set an intention that will change that structure and you can do this on many levels within your life. We are talking about the impersonal of the world but if you listen very carefully to what we are telling you, you will find all of this is playing out on a very personal level for you as well and why don't you heal and why don't you hold the power that you know you can hold and it is for the same reason that you witness in these other countries. You are carrying that cross, that burden within your own consciousness and creation and that is the new essence of your new age on this earth and this brings us back to that question of 12-12-2012, twelve, twelve, twelve or twenty-one, it is how you view it. Are you ready to make those shifts, are you ready to see yourself differently and work differently from within your framework and if you are, the you will make that transition through the 21st but we are again pulling numbers out of the air for in reality it is here today as it was yesterday and the years before, it is just now that you choose to see it, for there is nothing that has ever been placed on your earth that does not always exist, it is just where and how you see it and you will see it in your time and the others will see it in their time. This is why it takes, and the Universe created time relative to space and this is the realm that we exist in.

Q. (Mary) With the African situation, they are standing up against oppression but they don't really believe in themselves from within? Is this what you are saying?

This is so that you will understand that as a child stands and falls before it can learn to get its balance, there is no difference – the outpouring is the beginning point, that number 12 when you walk through that door but you will fall because it does not vibrate into the depths of the essence of creation yet. It still lives in the air, it is a thought that you are visiting so that you may get a sense of the ultimate direction that you follow. As that child stands up and takes a step and pops back down on their bottom, they will get back up again and they may flounder and they may end up on their bottom, us on that vibrational link with them, we are the strength, the thought and the belief to pick them up, we are that, we give them that but we give them nothing and so they move as would perceive as forward in time to fight another day.

This gentleman that is oppressive has been brought to them by them and he is not a villain in this, he is the brightest light and in his way he is master of the dominion, a leader and we should revere and love him for what it is he is willing to do for those people for one man taking on his shoulders the weight of change on that level is truly a master and yet this is not how you will see him and by doing that you will actually disengage the progress that could be made because you put that power, that energy, that focus – please be aware that you do this through your whole life and you are meant to do this – this is your spiritual unfolding – this is how you get to know yourself. We do not ever judge, we merely point out from our side what it is that you can do to best get to know you and so therefore you can send your intention as arrows to us that strengthens those people but ultimately will strengthen yourself – for you see it in others they are mirroring this to you.

Q. (Mary) Are you saying that it is not unlike the Hitler situation bringing an experience and learning to the whole world?

A marvellous gentleman, but we tend to glorify that and it has become a very spiritual, popular "coin a phrase" as you would say. He is merely the manifestation of that consciousness of the whole of the earth at that moment. They are the reflections of the people, they are the mirror - if that level of violence did not vibrate from within the masses, and how could that ever be brought into creation?

We could and we will in time open up the Hitler energy for remember with the physical death the Hitler energy did not leave the earth plane, the Hitler energy became the archetypal pattern for a way of being. You would call this the devil's way but it is not a devil as you would know it, it is a set of experiences, of consciousness, of growth and it is fertile and it is rich and we will speak more in time because through understanding these mass learnings that are so brightly highlighted to you, you will understand you for if you see it outside of the self, it is within the self that it originates.

Now this will be challenging, but this is our teaching, you wish to know how to help humanity, those last words were of the greatest assistance that could ever be given to the earth at any time but you have not matured just yet. With time, your time and with work you will understand this and we will work this so richly that you will truly become leaders upon your mountain that you stand and share this knowledge to all who wish to hear it for there will always be those who do not wish to hear that.

We are going to leave you with this thought – why are you creating so much illness in your society? Why do you feed your children poisons? Why do you feed yourself on hate? That is your diet of greed – where does this lie in your consciousness? If you wish to live and reconnect with who you are, these questions have to be addressed by all.

PAUL – July 18 2008

Q. (Mary) *The year 2012 - will there still be people here and if so, what type of human beings will there be?*

Exactly the same as there are today except what we have just spoken about, that is the change, that is the shift of the ages. We will speak about your Mayan calendar - the Divine Mother and the Divine Father, heavenly Mother and Father, we wish to present these powers to you. The shift of consciousness is when the two merge as one, all of what we have spoken about, the consciousness, this shift and this calendar depicts it, your tarot cards have the sequence laid out, the Cross of Hende has the secrets laid out, the Star, the Moon, the Sun and Judgement, Judgement is the outcome.

2012 - there will be no external shift, this shift is internal, it is the magnetic base resonance that pulsates throughout your body, it is your conscious change, it is the release of the ego, it is lead into gold, materialism, egoism, selfism into the golden age and to that golden age of unity and oneness and we might give this to you today - when do these times overlap, when do they become fluent? When the crystals energy was birthed into the earth, there was prophecy for many hundreds of years throughout the Judaic trees of life and the wisdom of Kabbalah, Zolah, Zohar, they were speaking of this power long before it came and yet it came and was unrecognised because it came to teach us the power of heaven was within you. At the shift of the age into the Golden Age, all of the earth will become one and it is happening today, it is happening tomorrow, it is happening with every conscious thought with every person who believes that you can survive after you die, that you can speak as I do with you today with a being from a far different reality of consciousness. I am around all of the time but I do not choose to impinge myself and my patterns of thought onto the medium but I am in existence, I do not just cease to exist because I am separate from this body that can match the vibrational connection.

You are the shift of the ages, you are the New Age, your children are the expression for the future into the New Age and in Jesus' time, in Buddha time, in Krishna time but learn your disciplines - learn your disciplines, we urge you, for the journey within takes you into separation, it takes you into the depths of your soul and of who you truly are. With this power you will then be learning to be unresponsive to externals in your life and then you really understand the power of separation from the externals and impartiality to the outcome - now you have the discipline of the Master and it is the Master power and energy that brings the shift of consciousness to the masses on the earth as your Christ, your Buddha, your Vedic texts tell you, your Zohar, your Bible, all of your sacred texts, the Koran, they all have this element contained within their scripture.

You are not a human form to me and yet I see you as radiant light, you are a pattern of thought, no more and no less. You are light frequencies and a vibration, you are beautiful and eternal, magnificent, you are a diamond, perfection - we do not understand why you do not see this beauty.

Paul – July 24, 2008

Q. (Mary) Are you able to tell us about earth changes in the next five years and also the changes within us?

I have already been telling you this if you would learn to listen to who you are. We will put it like this with the earth changes – there is that pattern that we have been describing to you as mass, who you are is the stream of energy, of light that breathes light and spirit and action, we come to action.

All of what you are, and please keep in mind that pattern formation that comes together to weave the solid mass so that the spirit, the pattern of light can connect through the mass and through the mass, action is put upon the earth. At any time you can change the light and you can shift the vibration which will shift the outcome. The more of you who do this with the same purpose, the same action and intention of the action, the movement forward, then you will change the outcome. The outcome is variable, we come back to the opposites, the smallest holds the most power, the smallest action, like the smallest point of the Universe contains the whole of this universal pattern. The smallest action contains the largest change, you perceive that it must be en masse but we say that the individual intention is the biggest point of action and movement which change the outcome and it is not something that will be in your conscious mind, it will be a shift, it will be the universal shift as to what you become and what do you become? You become more finely tuned to that light, you vibrate further back along the light beam and you have a far finer understanding of your consciousness.

The mass, the physical manifestation changes density, there is more light and the light is brighter, therefore the expression of that light has a different intention to the action so the outcome in that instant changes, the intention sent to you at this time is that of change. You are now peeling back the layers of time into that point of awareness of just how timeless you are – from that perspective you see yourself more clearly. When you are far denser in nature as you have been for eons on your earth, slowly the origin of your anatomy is changing to cope with the frequency of your spirit and memory of who you are. As this consciousness shifts your weight, you are pulling your body into alignment. The light becomes brighter; the intention changes from self awareness, greed, anger to a far more harmonious peace.

We would urge the path to least resistance, you will feel the resistance as that anger, that ego, that self, that selfishness, the other side of selfish is selfless and this is who you are, you just have not managed to access that part of you but as you become more selfless you will change where you are working from, you will become more harmonious to the people who are around you, you will align to their vibration far more than you have ever had before. So separation from all on the earth as individuals will mass as a collective unity, now this is where you will being that power of the individual into the manifestation of the masses. When the manifestation of the masses starts to work in harmony with the planet, you will affect the changes but the changes have already begun. You will now deal with the consequences of the selfishness because you have become so selfish that you cannot become the unity of selflessness to affect change fast enough to affect the physical outcome of that expression, the sound between the notes, the feelings within your heart is representative of the feelings that are woven into your earth.

Your mountains are alive, your trees are alive, the rock formations are alive, the animal kingdom has life, it has its own particular light vibrational pattern and we ask that you live from a place of respect. The planet is mirroring back to you who you are and the mirror is saying that you are selfish, you are greedy, you do not respect, you are bottomless vacuums that cannot be filled and when we say that point of the Universe that we are all connected to, please understand that the very earth that supports you, if you could see the vibration, the gravity, the forces of the Universe, the matrix you have called it on the earth, the Cosmic sheet, the blueprint, you would see that light moving from like a shooting star back through the eons of time into that infinitesimally small point of the centre of your Universe. So when you are harming, taking, digging, killing, you may as well put a gun to your own head for when you harm a tree without reverence for its life force, it is your life force that you are killing – how can it not be?

This is what is meant by saying that we are formless, we are non-sensory, we are non-weight, there is no mass – we are all one essence and that essence is truly light and this is why we say the spark of life, the candle in the dark, because that is who you are. We want you to know this, for if you truly knew this, you would not do what you are doing but why do you come to the earth in the first place but to remember and before you can remember you have to forget and it is an unconscious transition to consciousness and that is what your whole life is. It can be summed up in just that sentence, from consciousness to unconsciousness to consciousness, from awake to asleep but do not think that you wake up just because you pass over back to spirit for you do not truly wake up – it is like you are in suspended animation, you are conscious as in a dream and then you do the next round until you come back to the dream.

You do not fully awaken the whole of who you are, you do not fully access the light beam until you have come to finalisation of the physical life that you have been living and you view this life as your time on the earth through one cycle but we say that your life is through the millions of cycles and what are you actually learning? You are learning mastery of the self, you are learning how to contain this force that vibrates within that dense weight, you are learning how to connect again with who you are, you are bit by bit peeling back the layers of sleep that is in your eyes, you are coming into alignment, you are becoming the master of your being. As you become the master through this much lived life, you then become more selfless in your nature, you will become of the earth but you will never be contained by the earth as your interest in the earthly beings and happenings will no longer be the currency of your life, you will want the currency of what you can give to life for it is that currency that you are awakening throughout all of your life and that currency is your God force. So when somebody who is an individual expression of self betrays you, you will not wish to be angry at them, that emotion no longer lives within your being. You will wish to thank them for you are mastering your own emotions. There are the elements that are contained within you, earth, fire, wind, water, mind, breath, all of these elements intention, all of them, are who you are.

Q. *(Alex) I have heard of the celestial hierarchies – would you like to speak on that please?*

Celestial hierarchy – they are those who have awoken from this sleep, they have lived the lives that you have lived, they have done their deeds and they have awoken from that dream that you are living at this time. Remember we said that the vibration of the earth is connected to the centre of the All, remember we have said that the Universe is all space and expansive and infinitesimally large, remember we have said that the Universe has planetary masses of consciousness in this tapestry. The Masters, the celestial Masters who you are speaking of, they have gone through the cycles of birth and death and resurrection as your Master Christ has done.

The earth has had many vibrations that have been contained within that time back to eternity and each eon of time has manifested in a different vibration so you may like to look at it like this – there is the centre point of the nothing and the All, there is the beam of light, the candle, the light in the dark that shone forth, from this the beams of light shot out, shot forth into birth and creation over eons, more eons than you could ever contemplate, there was a different light frequency which contained different masses of energy. Each of these energies all were congruent as one and yet were all individual in nature. They all manifest through time, each time connected to the one preceding it, moving forward through the eons as the Universe expands. There is nothing that was created that is not in manifestation now so throughout this eon of creation, from the very first vibrational light mass, the Masters, the people, the vibrational spark that was created in that vibrational escrow, that is still playing to this day – you are just further along the blueprint and the further away from the centre mass, the more physical the being. As you reach critical mass you will then move back into alignment with the next transcendent eon of time.

The next transcendent eon of time will take you back through the cycle as we move back into that connection to the Source. Each Master has an element of awareness of mastery from that dimensional pull, they are all working in this time and yet they are all independent in their own time – they call this superposition, many, many aspects of the same consciousness so they are not separate from you but they are separate of you, they are a higher reflection of the mirror and so they come together over the eons of time and collective memory, the brain pattern which is the pattern in your own individual brain. That is the point that they access to give recognition to who they are, they then come in on that vibration and you have to mentally perceive them as do all spiritual aspects of the Divine Creator Universe. You see this through the point that you know as vision but you do not see it through the point of the eye – look at the paradox of how you view the world, when you are given physical vision, you see it through the back of your head, it starts at the back and moves to the front. This vision of the Masters starts from the front and moves to the back and reflects back to that mirror – this is how you see them and they come to help you to become aware and to wake up the consciousness within you – the memory of who you were, the lives that you have lived over these eons of time.

PAUL – July 31, 2008

Q. (Mary) When we progress earthbound spirits in our group, what happens when they are reconstructed?

The reconstruction of the spirit is the spirit who is living in ignorance, it has forgotten who it is, it has forgotten its essence, it has forgotten its incarnation – when you have moved it on, it has been sitting fully in this consciousness. When we reconstruct the spirit, we take it into the full soul of that individual aspect, the full soul is all of the parts that have been incarnations over eons, it is the wardrobe of experience, it is the part of it that is immortal, it is that part of it that was living thousands of times over and over as it is woven into this soul group, this soul experience.

Now we shall take it further and we shall say that every spirit who has contacted that particular energy has also got its own wardrobe, this then becomes part of the extension of that wardrobe so it gets reconstructed by the very essence of all of its parts coming into wholeness. As this spirit transcends from the limitations of the physical life and it is brought into the light, it is held in what you would call a hospital but not in the sense that you would have a hospital, it is in repair but it is not in repair because it is ill, it is in repair because it has forgotten who it is and it is holding onto fear, the fear from the earth and it is in ignorance of the expansion of the entire soul group. So we hold it in a place where it is a vibrational match, this then slowly but surely reconstructs and places the energy within that consciousness and it is like a cellular memory that is being re-awoken, this may take in your linear time a long time but in the spiritual aspect it will be instantaneous, they are merely in ignorance of who they are.

When they are reconstructed they then have the memory of that life, of all life, of all parts, of all beings, of all self, then they are reconstructed and then they will choose the time and the place within the construct of the woven tapestry of the other life and how they all serve themselves and intermingle. You will understand that there is not one person who you will meet on the earth plane who is not an extension of this soul grouping and as much as there are many, think of it like when you see a cell and you see it in the science laboratory, a molecular structure and it has bits that come off and then it has the circles as it builds from the main structure. This you would call the cosmic infinity, all of the offshoots are the little sparks that come off to make that soul grouping and every single one of them comes to the main source in the middle, so you can never be separate from the source, however when you have been very plugged into your earth life and you have forgotten who you are it can take time.

Unfortunately on the earth you do not allow your souls freedom with consciousness, you quite often pass over onto the spirit side of life with still your full awakening and awareness being from where you came because you have to go through the separation of the soul group so that you may get the experience that you need on the earth plane. This is then where you will set up your script again with that consciousness of that circle part of the whole and you will come back in as a woven tapestry and you will experience all that you have experienced and have not worked through to finalisation and this is where you will encounter those fears.

Does this answer your question? Yes, thank you for all of the information that you have brought through.

We are very happy to oblige in this for we know that there is a lot of information that has been placed on the earth and we wish to have our voice because we feel that we can help you as you go through this new awareness and awakening. The whole of your conscious group is starting to awaken and we are very pleased to see this happen and we do hope that this information will become the mainstay of how you live your life. If you understand who you are, you will speed up the maturation process and you may even avoid what you are very quickly drawing to your conscious experience and what you are drawing is not a very pleasant one from your side on the physical, although from our side we do not really care one way or the other – it is merely an experience that you are choosing.

Lilong Li – August 29, 2008

Q. (Mary) Your group has spoken of opposites, the dark side and the afterlife – my question is about those who have come to the earth to teach great lessons to their community and often to the whole world, when they return to the afterlife do they have to confront the havoc and dark side that they brought with them?

We have already answered this when we spoke about the one, the great soul who created the holocaust and cost more souls in one fell swoop, for this soul this is his path and yes he will have to look, reflect, acknowledge, see all that has been created, it is not possible not to do this but there is no judgement. This person who chooses this weight, this journey into the earth, this chaos, this darkness, this has been a task of the work of many lifetimes and it is the finalisation of the process but if the earth was not a match for this being then it could not happen. There has to be a matching plane for this to occur, a straight playing field, there has to be a consciousness where this act can take hold.

This whole afternoon of speaking is about this very subject for this very subject is your soul's journey from the sacred side so for all of the evil that you perceive, we would say that the highest masters who have come have also brought light but in the light that they brought in this time of the birth they experienced chaos for in the moment of the living, in the ego, in the serving for the self alone, this is the very essence of the soul's journey, this is why they have incarnated and they will feel the emotion in the heart, they will have the questions and the fears for they are going through the process as all others are going through the process of life.

Once away from the earth, from limitation of the body, in the fullness of their soul, it becomes impersonal, it does not matter for they have fulfilled the need of the masses in the incarnation of that time and so they are truly God's Angel, they are God fulfilling each other's needs. There is no separation, you are born as innocent, pure God and you return to pure innocence God.

Q. (Alex) A friend of mine was recently told that human illness is directly related to genetics – I find it difficult to agree with that comment – would you comment on the relationship between human illness and genetics please?

When being born into a body, temporal, the temple, you need a structure for your soul, your family unit, your blueprint, your genealogy; this is the very fabric and the temporary position of your incarnation and all hinges. When we spoke about coming into the earth blind, when we speak about being born into a body that has a genetic default, when you are born in to this it is by your soul's design, you have chosen each parent for the genetic factor that is going to be expressed in the next generation. The haemophiliac chooses the two parents who meet, who will turn on the genetic fault as the two genes meet in the creative process but they still have the option as to whether to finish that incarnation, this is where we say that the soul can redefine and choose to come home through the miscarriage or the termination of that life.

Your genetic structure can be used on many levels for a child being born into the earth it is not always genetics that cause the illnesses for children. From the moment the child is born and placed into the mother's womb at conception, that entity is like a sponge, it is picking up the vibration of the people it is coming to join. The people who it is coming to join and experience life with, what they are believing, their actions, the way they choose to live the experience through the ego, this is directly sent into that sponge and the programming for beliefs in the physical incarnation is ignited. Now the child is born and is programmed and indoctrinated in to that belief structure and the genetic code is like switches and the switches of experience, the experiences are felt in the emotional body, the emotional body carries the triggering factors, the stimuli, the hormones, the chemical responses to the light and front of the body and then receptors meet with the receivers in the genetic blueprint of the child – the genetic blueprint of the child is then activated.

So you, Sir have a certain genetic weak disposition and some character strength position and through external beliefs and behaviours when you were being created and when you were in that stage of vulnerability, that is what determines which receptors and receivers match and it is the emotion, the heart, the feeling that will determine if the haemophiliac will be created, if the Downs' Syndrome will be experienced, if the muscular diseases and degeneration will be ignited for that is the condition and some experience will be set about the possibility of being born blind, or losing vision at a certain age is also tied in with this blueprint and for the plan of the life as to what will serve the soul in that moment.

So a child may choose the genetics that will be on hold for three years, they may seem ordinary and have all the faculties of a normal child and at that age because of external experiences of the people within the life, that child may elect to become blind, to lose hearing at that age and so that shall be. What you are asking is so varied and so deep, it would take a level of understanding of the individual of each experience that is being incarnated through each family – there is no one answer for each child born of the earth comes in with a mixture of all of that which has been discussed here today. I hope that answers your question.

Father Bartholomew – September 11, 2008

Q. (Mary)   The argument about abortion or termination has been raging on for many years, is it true that the incoming spirit knows of this decision beforehand?

From when I was on the earth through the incarnation of Bartholomew, I would have said that you were committing a murder to take any life but that would merely have been a judgement from my own perspective and belief structure, my perceptions - this is a two-fold question and there are layers to it. The two souls before incarnation, both mother and child, on one level will have already made a pact, an agreement that they will be mother and child for if this was not so the two could not incarnate in the same sphere, into the same body.

However, there is also the level where the mother at the time, because of the external, because of the situation, her life has taken her to. When in spirit the program was that of perfection but at that certain point they would meet again on the earth plane but what they did not count on perhaps were the choices that the mother has made from the time of the incarnation beginning to the point of agreement. If the mother has made different choices in the ignorance of the plan, forgetting why she has incarnated and has lost contact with that inner resource, that inner spring, then she will find it very hard to be in the place where she may have foreseen her life making the choices that would have brought her to the point of union with that little soul and so when they meet and the soul comes in that has been organised, the mother has the divine right to turn to the child and to say "dear little one we are of one soul and for this moment in your time and my life I return you back to God's hands and I do this with love for I do not feel that I have made the choices that have brought me to this state where I can manage to have the child". With that agreement, the child in its perfection most times will spontaneously break that silver cord of connection with its spirit and then the body will die and so there will be no damage from the child's side but all too often because of the external perceptions, beliefs and morals that are placed in your society and those who stand on the moral high ground, the mother feels like a murderer and carries the guilt wave through the biology and this is toxic, therefore the mother becomes unwell and grief stricken.

To celebrate union, to celebrate and honour both lives, the mother is projected as the incubator where we came in this afternoon, the mother has no right in your society and yet from our side, the mother is the very essence of the baby being born into the life for the mother's perspective is what determines the biology and the experience of that babe – she is the one who ultimately knows what is best for her in that moment, in that choice, so the honouring of the spirit is what we would say would be productive.

You have some interesting ideas upon your earth and I myself have had many an incarnation where I have taken the moral high ground, it is a part of being human, it is a part of incarnation.

Is there anything else that you wish to discuss this afternoon?

Q. (Alex)   I have read recently that in this current age our DNA structure is going through cellular changes, would you like to comment on that – perhaps we are mutating into a different species?

It is not that you are mutating into a different species for man has always been man, it is the electromagnetic pulse that is changing. You are recognising yourself as computers, you are incoming and you are a program and you are outgoing, we would liken it to a wave of energy through your cellular structure when we break it down to its smallest factor and it is empty and is merely an electrical charge, there is the strong atom, there is the weak part of the atom and when the two collide, you get the nuclear explosion.

This is the electromagnetic field, this is the chi, this is the life force in motion, you must be in motion to be alive, if you are not in motion then you are dead. It is not so much that the DNA is changing for this is not truly possible for as long as you are a body you need the same essence, you need the same amino acids, proteins and building blocks that make the cellular structure, it is the source that moves the cellular structure that changes and we shall describe it like this – if you were to drop a pebble on the water you will get a ripple but the ripple is not moving the water, what is actually moving to create the ripple is the electrical charge, the wave, the movement of the two essences colliding.

So if you had a fishing line with a buoy, it would not move the buoy, the wave would just lift it and move past it. Now is you were to drop another pebble slightly after the first, then that pebble would drop down and create a secondary wave, it is when the two waves collide that they cancel each other out, this is what is happening with your life force, you have been living on a frequency, you have been living on a pulse, this pulse has been governed by the magnetic polarisation of the planet that you live on. The heartbeat pulses through the body and creates the pressure for your body and your blood to move, it is the same as the analogy of the pebble. When you lift the wave and the wave becomes higher, those that cannot lift to that height of the wave, then it is drawn into the higher pulse, it is a bit like having a light globe, a 20 watt globe is outshone by a 100 watt bulb, these two waves, the light that is 100 will literally cancel out the 20 watt globe. This is what is happening in your cellular structure, you are vibrating and there are parts of you that are vibrating higher than other parts of the people on the earth, so we have entities working at 20 volt, 30 volt, 40 volt, 100 volt and the vibes that are being sent out by the 100 volt is shining and cancelling out the energy of the 20 watt bulb and drawing it up into its very essence.

At some point and we would say in the heavens that when the Sun aligns with the centre of the Galaxy the waves will merge and the cellular energy construct of the quantum will then change – now you will be instantaneous, no time, everything happening in an instant, it will be a time of re-evaluating the way that you perceive and receive – this is the mutant changing. We would say to you that the body will not mutate any cells, the cells have a cancelling out program that stops this from happening, the cell that is mutating can only mutate if it is given a different vibration program, so the energy is lifted and the perception and program is changed.

The construct of your world changes to meet this higher awareness – do you understand what we have been discussing?

Lilong Li – September 25, 2008

Q. (Alex) I was thinking of a question yesterday and you answered it in your talk – have you been listening in?

I am always with you my dear friend and I am always in communication with you, always will and I am never separate from you. If you could see you through our eyes you would know this my dear beloved friend.

Q. (Mary) Does the entity who came through before have a name or isn't that important?

You know this entity and we do not give names, seek in your heart and you will know who this entity was, if you dare to believe then you will know.

Shishila 2 – October 9, 2008

Q. (Mary) I have found a village in India with the name of Shishila and there is a temple there built for the god Shishileshwara – does this have any relevance to the Shishila who speaks to us?

Shishila is merely a label that is placed on an energetic place in time, I embodied the energy of that time, there was a time that was birthed on the earth where there was a Goddess vibration of creation, that Goddess vibration of creation was created within the mist of the mind of the consciousness of the people of that time. They created a myth, they created ritual and they created that god energy and they placed the label Shishila on to that god energy, that god energy that lived in that time, they then revered and they lived through the ritualistic beliefs, they had to bring it into a place where they could manage it. It was not born of a time like today where you can really understand a formless form, they had to try to touch it, manoeuvre it and work it and pay lip service to that Goddess energy, the Goddess energy was of course for fertility, it was the creation of life that they were actually celebrating for to them this was a mystery of all mysteries – how did that child come from another being? The woman must have had some very powerful energy, spells and magic and so to revere that new creation was of the utmost and then they took to the fields for if they were to survive they needed food so they needed the fertility of the seed in the soil and they placed that god magic into the very fabric of the soil, they then created an expression of that reverence for birth and creation within the framework of the individual.

Shishila that you speak of is a more modern day lineage connected to that vibration and I have no problem with them using that name for Shishila is the Goddess of God energy, it is that creative force, there is no new God force on your earth only a different understanding of this so where Shishila, the name and the reverence for creation and the point of interest that is perceived as growth, that is what is created, reverence for life is adhered to, the streams are teeming with life, the surrounding fields are fertile because that space in time of consciousness, that is the reverence, the vibration that their consciousness pool of unified people worked within and so it had to be. However, if you took the name Shishila and placed it before another culture who have never really looked at that creative Divine force in that fertility energy, it would hold no power and they would not live that expression, they would have another way of doing it, like the Christian Church, like the esoteric Essenes, like the Indian, the native of America, like the Incas and the Andes and the Peruvian gods, like all of the different gods of the Tibetans, they all have that individual aspect of that but it may not necessarily be on the womb and fertility, it may be placed in a different space although it will be of the same God force.

Q. (Mary) In a recent session you mentioned the word Baal Shem Tov – would you explain to us what this means please?

The Baal Shem Tov is an individual lifetime brought through this medium – everything that we have been saying about the Shishila is also of the Baal Shem Tov energy but this is more patriarchal, it was taken through another door. The Master of the Baal Shem Tov was actually a Master who travelled through many, many countries and who brought enlightenment, not unlike the Buddha, not unlike the Krishna, they are just a less known vibration to those two fields of consciousness so you see that Master energy is expressed over many different eons of time. The Baal Shem Tov was the Master who was a seer, whereas other energies came in to teach on different levels, the Baal Shem Tov was the healer and was the seer vibration, which is the role of this medium. The Baal Shem Tov was revered in his time and was very much a Master and a wise sage in other terminology so when we say Baal Shem Tov, understand that this was a very powerful energy that lived on the earth, it was just lived before pen and paper and recorders, it was folklore and it was handed down from generation to generation and that generation has shifted so now they have an expression of a new re-working of that religious, that philosophy that you would recognise in the more Kabbalahistic philosophy of mysticism, the mysticism was born from this age of the Baal Shem Tov. As you have the Dalai Lama for the Tibetans, think of the Baal Shem Tov who year after generation and year after generation, the wisdom was passed on through that particular vessel which was that medium who brought that energy through into the world. I hope this helps to explain that term.

We feel that there are small nuggets regarding the Baal Shem Tov but they are deeply placed in the more mystical side of the Kabbalahic philosophy, through the Zohar[4] but it is not in the Zohar that has been written in the time that you would know, this is a very ancient practice of religion and mysticism and it really does precede your time of recognition of history on this earth so you may find this a hard piece of information to find today so we wish you well but we do believe that there are stories within, we will say like the layers of a cake, that within the stories that have been handed down, there are aspects of that person but do not look for a person as such for it was not just a person, it was like a system of priests as you would call it, holy ones, mystical beings. This is not to say that this particular person is anything other than totally normal, however she has had many expressions and is like an older soul in the scheme of incarnational processes.

Kukuwani – December 5, 2008

Q. (Alex) Before we incarnate, I have heard that we choose our parents and the people who will be around us – would you like to comment?

This is so, for if it were not so there would be no life on the earth. When you are not in form, you are the drop being placed back into the ocean; the main body of water is the spirit of all humanity, of the animal kingdom, of all of creation. It is the individual drop that separates for a short time, your mother before you, they are you, they know you, they know all of you and everyone on the earth, it cannot be other and when returned to Source you are returned to each other and everything that you have created is brought through the intelligence – you call it memory, we call it vibration and light, it is a sea of light.

---

4. **Zohar** – group of books written in Aramaic about the five books of the Torah. Shishila commented that this is a modern day Zohar. The ancient Zohar is Jewish mysticism and the Jewish Kabbalah.

When the light hits the prism, all of the colours of creation are visible but all of creation and the colours of creation are visible always, you just need the reflection, the light to see it separate from the entire mass surrounding it, a mother and a father serve that purpose, they are merely the reflection so that birth, life and individuation can be experienced, it cannot be other. Do you understand that truly?

Q (Alex). Some of us choose to have a very difficult life, would you comment on why we would do that?

Why wouldn't you? Nothing can ever harm you, it is merely that you perceive it to be hard from your limited perspective of separateness but if you listen to what we have already said, the perpetrators who take the life and the person whose life has been taken are in perfect harmony, it cannot be other or the two essences could not exchange that experience, it is the experience that you are here for - the physical form is just a way of achieving that end. When you are having difficulties in your life, celebrate for your life is working for your own growth, it cannot be other.

So my people came to the earth to be exterminated, it was their time and they agreed to have the perceived perpetrators at that specific time enter their consciousness and end that cycle and rhythm of life and yet we did not cease to exist, we are still fully present, we walk among you, we are you, we just chose the time when the culture, when the expression of that time and experience and way of living and belief structure would no longer serve to take us to that next level in our evolution. We had taken what we needed from the experience of that culture and when we came back to join with the body of water, we took all of the individual experiences of that culture built over generations and it became blended and a part of that essence of water. Now it is available to the very people who you would have perceived to be our victimisers, it cannot be other.

Q. (Alex) I understand about contractual agreements but I feel at a loss how to explain to those around me the purpose of their hardships or traumas that they may be going through.

You cannot – I can't help them? – no, it is not for you to do this, you can be a light that shines before them, you can never tell them, you have to show that, live it, the more who live it the more they can experience that and then reflect it back to you. You can never show anything that is not already in that pool and they are in that pool, the contract, the essence of who they are is not ready to become aware yet but by you understanding by living it, by breathing it, by knowing that truth, you reflect the pool of infinite knowledge to them and when they are ready, they embrace. You make it possible by you believing it.

Q. (Mary) Please tell us who is speaking with us today.

We are indigenous to the North American tribes, we lived in a place where there were extreme paradoxes from mountains so high that were covered with snow to valleys so lush that everything grew. You would not be able to pronounce my name but the name that I give you is Kukuwana.

Winston Whitehorse –December 18, 2008

Q. (Mary) Recently we have experienced a crash of the financial markets, the markets of greed etc. and we thought that this may be the beginning of great changes to come, unfortunately the Governments have rescued many of these institutions – in your opinion what is it going to take to bring about changes?

Maturation, it will take the introspection and it will take the change of the individual because even if those financial situations collapse, there will be many others to take their place. It is never going to happen as a global catastrophe or a global calamity because as soon as one crashes there is always another that will profit. What it will take, we will say it like this – it will start with the individual person, it starts within your home, it starts within your individual relationships and your relationships to each other, it starts with your values and your assets that you assign value to, it starts with the global belief and the global consciousness of giving and not receiving, it starts with all of these different elements, it can never start with a financial collapse. You must understand, every change that has ever been birthed into the earth starts with a few and as that few live that consciousness, then that few project that out and the people of like mind tap into that source and stream and as they tap into that source and stream then they project that out and then more can tap into that source and that stream.

That source and that stream is that of giving, is that of service and is that of not living a life of competition, survival of the fittest. Please understand where your global climate has actually come from, we would have to take you back to your time where you birthed into creation, you had a crossroads, a point in your evolution and we are coming back to the actual evolutionary debate and the argument that has been raging on your earth ever since. Survival of the fittest was what you chose to breathe life into and this will emanate and illustrate what we mean by a few to the next to the next, so one man gets a download and has an observation and says that if you look at animals or the animal kingdom, they are always constantly evolving to suit the situation that is around them and if one does not evolve to match the situation in the physical world around them to their best extent, then they will become extinct. If there are two species that are actually toe to toe, it is the one that can mutate and actually become stronger in the field of their environment and the other will then be extinguished.

You say this with homosapien and you say this with Neanderthal, it is rightly so on some levels but on that level that you brought into the earth, it was brought into the earth with the consciousness and the intention and the feeling that there was survival of the fittest, the weak must perish, it was brought into the earth on that vibration. Competition, survival of the fittest, we will continue to say this forever but it is not actually a truth, the truth of this is that it is never going to be a competition between the species but it will be compatibility, it will be conscious co-creating, it will be that energy of helping and nurturing and moving forward.

The mammalian species and time on your earth is that of nurturing and creating from one warm-bodied animal to another, that was the essence that was born when the mammalian cycle came onto the earth but you replaced that program with a new program, now that program of survival of the fittest became fascist. Your World War II was the catalyst for industrial expansion where the few, the oligarchy became powerful and then the weak perished and were drummed out of existence so you have the few barons who literally built all of the structures of modern commerce but it was not on mutual gratification, on mutual respect, it was on survival of the fittest and that competition and greed and profit.

This is when we have drawn the line in the past, the other energies who have come in before me and have drawn that line and said that the two lines on the earth had been meeting, flowing, expanding and reaching and in and out and intertwining and at that point they separated. The energy of who will you walk over to fulfil your own needs, selfishness, you will see it all over your world today, it is inbuilt, instantaneous gratification, that was the energy in that and we can trace it back to that person who came onto the earth and we will tell you that there was another who preceded him who had a very different structure and because he was not seen as having the right credentials and was not the right social class in a very socialistic society, that person took that work and then used the essence of what they needed to finish off their own work, then put it out and packaged it, then the other person is credited and he became the running joke.

It is only in today's climate that you are starting to understand that it is not survival of the fittest and we come down to the argument between intelligence design and evolution and we say that the two are closely linked and cannot be separated for both are true. As you rage the differences and try to prove the differences and argue and dialogue, you separate the power of the two, you separate the lines and the line that you ascend up becomes that of competition, greed, profiteering and that is what you have witnessed today, so it cannot be changed with a global financial meltdown for as it started hundreds of years prior with one person and it escalates, so shall it be again.

Those who do not have and feel least powerful plug into a system of order of spirituality and of Source and of recognising themselves as that Divine Source, this is the essence of that movement, of respecting, of looking at each other in communion. When this idea truly catches on and that Source energy and the idea emanates from the one to the two to the three and then that stream picks up, then there is a global financial meltdown yet again and there will be and it will continue to cycle until one day the popular culture through networking the stream from generation to generation to generation for those who are looking to expand spiritually, for those who are looking to understand themselves as Source, they pass that gift of selflessness onto the next generation by their actions, now that is truly karmic but you cannot change it for the Governments will always step in and the rich will get richer or so it will seem. Does this help to answer that question?

Q. (Alex) We were talking about karma, thought, feeling and actions - some people are described as quick tempered and act without thought and without feeling – would like to comment on that?

The energy that they in turn experience – we will put it in terms like the epicentre, the volcanic eruption, everything you see within you is a mirror to a physicality in your world, there will always be that dynamic, it cannot be other, so to truly give you an understanding on an in depth level of that, we will go into the centre of the earth. There is the world of emotion and emotionally charged, a lot of how you are brought up and brought into the world will determine what you have learnt and how to express yourself in the earth, how you respond to people, how you respond to situations, what you have been allowed to actually do and behave like, where you have been held accountable, where your boundaries have been set.

So think of the volcano and all of that energy building up within the very epicentre of the earth and that response, like a pull of hot fire, lava and over time, eons of time from the earth or a lifetime from infanthood, you have been taught to respond and react, respond and react, get your own way, control and manipulate, you feel the world, you sense the reaction, you feel the boundaries as they are set. when you meet resistance you will respond in kind, you will meet that response and if you are able to overpower and get your own way, then that sets up that program, no different from the earth building pressure, building pressure and it bulges – what do you think your hiatus hernias in your body are representing, your ulcers? That is also a manifestation of this behaviour and people who behave like that will actually have this dynamic going in, it may be in their stomach or maybe in their chest or wherever it is, they will have ulcerated intestines, wherever that control and that behaviour in that response mechanism, wherever that fire is sitting and underlying, the pressure builds, the pressure builds, the more the pressure builds the more the response, the more the response, the more the response builds, the quicker you react, the quicker you react.

Then at some point, snap, boom, the epicentre just flows from that beautiful stream of fire and emotion and the same is said for the physical body and then we will see murder, mayhem, chaos, road rage, it is up to you as individuals parenting, it is up to you as the individual to actually understand and set boundaries, this is what society is all about, this is why you have your collective experience, the collective dream, this is why you have your physical construct so that you are a measure to what is socially acceptable.

Now again we come into the social of the group and the individual family aspect, one family's response will not be the same as another, one family's programs will not run the same as another and the individuals within that framework are constantly being downloaded and interpreting what the rules of engagement are. Some become very placid and withdrawn because their nature in introverted but this does not mean that there will be that underlying, underlying, underlying seething and they are the ones you would say "butter wouldn't melt in their mouths" and then snap. Then you seem to have these ones who are forever kicking, screaming and loud and audacious and you say they are extroverted so the archetypal profile is also meshed in with this and the characteristics that will be displayed, there will be warriors and then there will be saintly ones, nuns, nurses, healers. It is when the two meet that there will be an explosion because one will set a boundary and one will not respond well to that boundary.

Does this answer your question and are there any other questions?

None that I can think of right now but it has been a most enlightening afternoon and as usual we come away full of knowledge, enlightenment and understanding and we thank you so much for all of that.

Lilong Li – December 30, 2008

Q. (Mary) What really happens when we pass from the earth – do we still keep the same body if we want to?

Why would you, why would you need such a cumbersome vehicle, you would not wish it for it would be like a baby trying to carry a giant, cumbersome – explain please.

Q (Mary). When people come through with messages and when they are able to explain what they looked like, I was wondering if some people still go around with the same body as on the earth.

They can if they wish but it is not truly the same body for your body will be discarded and it will return to the earth, whether that is in ashes or in dust, you will return to the earth. Now what you are talking about is the memory of that life and yes, every part of that life in every moment can be realigned and that soul essence can rework that energy and create that image and they can create it very well and it will feel real and they can stay there for many, many centuries but ultimately it is a myth and it will be discarded for growth is inevitable, it is like two magnets meeting each other – boom, they join then that imagery is no longer necessary for the soul to progress.

Nothing that you have experienced in any life is ever lost and when a loved one comes to meet with you on the earth, they bring with them a memory which is alive in you, they bring with them a sense of wishing to connect and so it is only fair that they try to present an image that can be recognised by the individual on the earth with limited perceptive ability. It would make no sense to come and show themselves and activate a memory that the person could not recognise and some of them do that because they like that imagery, that is what it takes for them to manifest and project that form into the memory banks of the medium, the living bridge, they are in a place of misalignment – do you understand?

Q. (Alex) There are a number of entities coming through who bring us information in these sessions – are they all a part of the same soul group and do you have a curriculum set out or a set of instructions to bring messages through to us or is it haphazard?

Nothing is ever haphazard, we can assure you and we would like to dispel a myth, the soul group is the same core, there is no separation between each form, it is the same form that will come and address you, just as you see your face in the mirror every morning, however, lifetime after lifetime there are individual manifestations of that form and it is that imagery that we bring to you – this is also an extension of the question from the other one. So we tap into the many, many lifetimes of expression on the earth, individual lifetimes, for each lifetime experience has a building block effect of knowledge attained and in that which is relevant that energy brings that vibration to you, that knowledge for it was that essence that truly understood that part of the earth experience that we are bringing today but we bring it with the awareness of the whole of the soul group.

It is nice to introduce ourselves and it is nice, as was asked before, to remember who we have been in individual form for when we do this imagery and when we bring this into our being and we bring this to you, it is almost as if we live that life again and here is the next part of that question – yes, you are all a part of that soul group.

When we have someone who comes who has not been part of that soul group and the individual experience, you are understanding their personal lifetime karmic history, those who come through you will come through your experience on the earth for as much as we are all part of the soul group, we all have individual life experiences and lives to be lived on the earth. We bring all of that to the soul group but the individual life is that reincarnation, the reunification point of all of the lives, so when we bring through a life and a personality and a gender, we are merely activating a life that has already been experienced through that individual.

Q. (Alex) It is a fascinating business; I may have to go and sit on a mountain and contemplate my navel.

You have done that because the navel is the point of the karmic path of your life, that point holds every life that you have ever experienced and every relationship within every life, it is the karmic point of your being and it is very poignant that you sit on a mountain and ponder that point for who are you today but a composite of all that you were yesterday and of all that you will be tomorrow. All of those threads are all connected through that navel, the umbilical cord of creation and you have done this, you have sat, you have spent time on one of the highest mountains and you have been the hermit and you have pondered deep truths.

Unfortunately in the life that you chose to do that, you did not live physically to bring that back to the masses, you actually passed within that context of that cave in that mountain that you perched yourself upon for the world was not ready for that level of truth to be shared and so you elected to go home. You will meet this person as you develop but first we would suggest that you allow the personality that is driving the vehicle today, you must release that part of the ego if you wish to meet the composite of who you are and you will meet them in your navel.

Baal Shem Tov – January 8, 2009

Q. (Mary) In our last session you made mention that the entities coming through could be connected to our soul group and previous lives so those entities who we call our guides are they also our former lives?

They are personalities you have lived and experienced on the earth plane, they are your past lives, they are the ones who you most attach to in this experience and that is true.

Thank you – were we speaking with Baal Shem Tov today?

This is so, also be aware all who are part of this soul group have led some absolutely ordinary lives and has come from the lowest of the low and has led some of the most horrific and yet most joyful life experiences but she will not bring those through for they do not serve the purpose of this meeting. You have all led interesting lives.

Q. (Mary) You have spoken at length about karma and also about contracts, therefore is murder a part of a contract?

There is never a random act that is carried out in the field of the earth, even if you perceive it as an accident, there is always the energy that is outpouring, the ripple that is drawing that experience to you. As you have spoken about vertical time in the past, you will understand that every possibility is available to you, every possibility and experience at any time, your beliefs and what you are living they are the connectors to the experience. So if you come into the earth with the possibility of having had this experience in the past karmic connection but you wish to address and work through it, everything that you have done up until that moment where the murder or the perceived murder has taken place, now this is what we call the karmic line because these are all the elements that bring it to a higher possibility of that happening. However, if you have just changed one element of the life, one element of your response and reactivity, one element of the dynamics and emotion, then you will understand that although that person who may commit murder in one experience will walk straight past you for the glue that binds no longer serves, so like two ships in the night, you meet, you look and then you move away.

However, if you live a life that has been drawing that experience to it by taking by greed, by becoming manipulative, by fearing, by fearing your own shadow, by believing that you will be killed, by believing that you could be killed, then you electrically, magnetically draw that person into your field. It may seem random yet we say that it is not random for that person could not come to you if you did not emit the charge that says "I am now a vibrational match, this is a possibility, this is the experience and my life will finish here" for you will play the perpetrator and I will play the victim. In the past you may have had an experience, perhaps not with that energy that you meet in that moment, perhaps you have had the experience with the energy of a different vibration but those are the two who will meet and match that transaction at that moment and so it shall be done.

Now there are elements where it can only be accompanied by two people who are meeting at that moment and they must engage in that process because that is what it takes to bring that particular experience into reality. There are always variations and movements, there is never anything written in stone – does this help to explain this?

Q. (Mary) Yes, thank you but what of the supposed commandment "thou shalt not kill"?

This was brought through the mind of man, this was brought through reason and logic, justice and injustice and as long as you are always looking through your justice program of what you perceive to be right and wrong, then murder will always seem wrong. However, we say to you do not go out and commit murder, it is not the thing that you would do if you were truly trying to ascend to your higher purpose of your soul but we would say to you that in committing that murder you will then set up a charge and the rest of the experiences will meet you on that charge but not because we feel that it is right or wrong or injustice but because there is a fundamental law of the Universe that you do not have the right to interfere with anybody's progress at any time. If you are to interfere, then you are working with manipulation and you are serving yourself so selfishness is the private agenda and so you can see what that will bring to your life, the vibrational match in time and space that will bring experience back to you to teach you that perhaps you could do it differently, perhaps you could be wiser, perhaps you could be more forgiving – do you understand?

Q. (Alex) I find these talks so inspirational that I am inspired now to spend more time being in touch with my former selves – do you have any suggestions as to the best way to go about this process of getting in touch?

You can never be out of touch, now doesn't that just put a different spin on it, the only way that you can be out of touch is if you are not in alignment to Source so we would suggest that you work to bring alignment into your soul.

A lot of the time on your earth plane you spend ten minutes in your day and we will break it into incremental time because you understand that language but you give your attention for ten minutes or however long to your spiritual journey to who you are. You try to cram all of what you need to know into that time space and then you go about living your life and we would suggest to you that you live your life and then that is what makes you in alignment with your spirit. You must bring your spirit into alignment with your life, you must live your spirituality every moment of your day, it must become your language, when you speak the language fluently, you will speak the language of your spirit and then you cannot not meet the essence of what you are and you cannot not have that on tap. If you can manage that level of remembrance and knowing it will meet you in every area of your life but first you must live that, it must be you, it is the spiritual journey, it is everything that we have been speaking about today, it is the remembrance of who you are – you are the holy of the holy, you are majestic and you are infinite, you are magic, you are beauty personified, you are the rays of the heavens and the earth, you are golden in nature, you are divine and delicious, it is separation and the veil.

So I will give you the picture again – I will wrap you in a cosmic blanket, I will take away your individuality, the sense to perceive your physical form, what you look like, your movement and your senses and I will wrap you in this blanket and I will place you in the middle of all of your soul's lives for that is who you are. You work with your Tarot, you know the picture of the cups, this is you in the centre, all of your lives are all around you all of the time, it is who you are in the mix and the blend of personality supreme but you are blinded by the limitations placed upon the senses.

If you peel back that veil, if you go within and open to the majesty of who you are, if you stand in your light and you learn to manage your spirit, you will go into a knowing and remembrance so magical that you will be drunk upon the earth with joy. You will lift the veil of separation and transcend limitation and then you may not wish to come back to the earth at all but work from within, the sphere we work with today – do you see who you are, who you all are?

Pro-activity instead of reactivity, contain your expectations, live only for the minute, the moment, be truly a force unto yourself, honour who you are, go within and hear the unheard voice of your soul, give up control of the world around you and the people in it, unplug from ritual and ceremony, unplug from the global consciousness of morality, judgement, right, wrong, indifference, birth, death, all of the cosmic forces that keep you blind and in this veil for that is the essence and the tapestry of the veil of separation, that is what your Christ was, contain your light and be a wonder to behold and they too will write books about you.

HISTORICAL

Shishileshwara Temple

Shishila, though a remote village in Dakshina Kannada has a significant place for its sheer natural beauty coupled with healing powers of God Shishileshwara. The Mahashir fish in the Kapila River and the natural beauty around picturesque Shishileshwara temple can lighten anyone's burdened heart and drooped shoulders.

Shishila is at about 110 kilometres away from Mangalore and it comes under the jurisdiction of Beltangady taluk. From Beltangady one has to travel via Uppinangady (which is located at National Highway 48) and Kokkada. It may be a tedious journey and the path may be lengthy. But the mesmerizing natural beauty and fish in the fish sanctuary would not disappoint anyone.

The fish in the sanctuary at Shishila are believed to be sacred and Naive yam is offered to them after offering pujas.

There are two rocks in the river. While one is 'Huli Kallu' (rock named after tiger), the other is called as 'Dana Kallu' (rock named after cow). According to mythology, a tiger and a cow reached the river when tiger chased the cow. But God did not want violence. Hence, he converted tiger and cow into rocks. The rocks do wear the looks of cow and tiger. During the annual feast (Jatre), pujas is offered for both the rocks.

According to the historians, the Shishileshwara temple, which is located on the banks of river Kapila, has a history of more than 800 years. Every year, annual feast is held here at the end of May and it lasts for 9 days, with the support of locals who mostly reside in the close vicinity of the temple.

According to the temple sources, pilgrims throng in big numbers from January and May. Many devotees come here with offerings for fulfilling their wishes. They also enjoy watching fish in the river and feed them with rice, beaten rice and puffed rice. While watching these fishes and natural beauty here, one can forget all the miseries of life. Shishila indeed has that power. The freedom, love and care experienced by fish here is perhaps something which is very unique to this place only.

God Shishileshwara

Baal Shem Tov

Rabbi Yisroel (Israel) ben Eliezer August 27, 1698 (18 Elul) to May 22, 1760, often called Baal Shem Tov or Besht, was a Jewish mystical rabbi. He is considered to be the founder of Hasidic Judaism (also Mezhbizh Hasidic dynasty). Besht was born to Eliezer and Sara in Okopy, Ternopil Oblast a small village that over the centuries has been part of Poland, Russia, and is now part of Ukraine. He died in Medzhybizh, which had once been part of Lithuania, then Turkey, Poland and Russia, and is now in Ukraine.

Besht is better known to many religious Jews as "the holy Baal Shem" (der heyliger baal shem in Yiddish), or most commonly, the Baal Shem Tov. The title Baal Shem Tov is usually translated into English as "Master of the Good Name", with Tov ("Good") modifying Shem ("[Divine] Name"), although it is more correctly understood as a combination of Baal Shem ("Master of the [Divine] Name") and Tov (an honorific epithet to the man). The name Besht — the acronym from the words comprising that name, bet ayin shin tes—is typically used in print rather than speech. The appellation "Baal Shem" was not unique to Rabbi Yisroel ben Eliezer; however, it is Rabbi Yisroel ben Eliezer who is most closely identified as a "Baal Shem", as he was the founder of the spiritual movement of Hasidic Judaism.

The little biographical information that is known about Besht is so interwoven with legends of miracles that in many cases it is hard to arrive at the historical facts. From the numerous legends connected with his birth it appears that his parents were poor, upright, and pious. When he was orphaned, his community cared for him. At school, he distinguished himself only by his frequent disappearances, being always found in the lonely woods surrounding the place, rapturously enjoying the beauties of nature. Many of his disciples believed that he came from the Davidic line tracing its lineage to the royal house of King David, and by extension with the institution of the Jewish Messiah

The Eye of Horus (Wedjat); previously *Wadjet* and the **Eye of the Moon;** and afterwards as the Eye **of Ra** or **Udjat** is an ancient Egyptian symbol of protection and royal power from deities, in this case from Horus or Ra. The symbol is seen on images of Horus' mother, Hathor, and on other deities associated with her.

Horus was an ancient Egyptian sky god in the form of a falcon. The right eye represents a Peregrine Falcon's eye and the markings around it, that includes the "teardrop" marking sometimes found below the eye. As wadjet (also udjat or utchat), it also represented the sun, and was associated with Horus' mother, Isis, and with Wadjet another goddess, as well as the sun deity Ra. The mirror image or Left eye sometimes represented the moon and the god Tehuti (Thoth).

EPILOGUE

And so ends book one, Unity of Consciousness, a compilation of information and knowledge from the world of spirit, brought forward by those in higher realms through the amazing trance mediumship of Carol Crawford.

Book two is under way and it is proving to be as exciting and informative as book one, not only that but book two is an extension of book one and expands on the knowledge gained from book one, and old friends return along with new friends. We now call them friends for that is what they have become.

The Pearls of Sophia Wisdom
Sacred Connections through the whispers of time

In book two "The Pearls of Sophia Wisdom" you will embark on the more intimate aspects of your incarnational process, The personal blueprint of your soul's identity and what makes you respond in your life to the situations, people, and the karmic charge between you and your personal relationship entanglements. Using some of the most ancient teachings ever embraced on earth and by applying these teachings in the expansion of who you are as essence and source energy. You have come to know yourself as merely a physical body. Now unravel your energy anatomy using the seven Essene Mirrors of Reality. By applying this technological and psychological power tool to understand the essence of experience and the reflection that experience has created within your own cosmic fingerprint you begin to open the gateway of understanding your own nature and the individual characteristics.

By understanding the seven energy centres located within your physical body along with that reactive and responsive mechanistic aspect of you <u>emotional body</u> and weaving in the Essene Mirrors of Reflection and learning the symbolic language of the Eighth energy centre, "<u>your spiritual body</u>", the tapestry of past present and future begin to unravel and the directive force of your spirit is revealed as you paint the cosmic painting which is that timeless aspect of your eternal spark; it's the unlimited potential and divine spark that is at the core of all of your individual characteristics.

OTHER PRODUCTS FROM THE AUTHOR

Web Site: carolcrawford.com.au/
Email: carolcrawford20@optusnet.com.au
PO BOX 10084
L.P.O PINES FOREST
FRANKSTON NORTH 3200
VICTORIA
AUSTRALIA

Disc Cover Artwork (TURINE)
By Laura Floyd
Copy rights 2009 All Rights reserved